W9-BTD-058

PLAYS FOR PERFORMANCE

*A series designed for
contemporary production and study
Edited by
Nicholas Rudall and Bernard Sahlins*

ANTON CHEKHOV

The Cherry Orchard

In a New Adaptation by
Robert Brustein

Based on a Translation by
George Calderon

Ivan R. Dee

CHICAGONEW HANOVER COUNTY
PUBLIC LIBRARY
201 CHESTNUT STREET
WILMINGTON, N C 28401

THE CHERRY ORCHARD. Copyright © 1995 by Ivan R. Dee, Inc. Adaptation copyright © 1995 by Robert Brustein. All rights reserved, including the right to reproduce this book or portions thereof in any form. For information, address: Ivan R. Dee, Inc., 1332 North Halsted Street, Chicago 60622. Manufactured in the United States of America and printed on acid-free paper.

CAUTION: Professionals and amateurs are hereby warned that this edition of THE CHERRY ORCHARD is subject to a royalty. It is fully protected under the copyright laws of the United States of America and of all countries covered by the International Copyright Union (including the British Commonwealth and Canada), and of all countries covered by the Pan-American Copyright Convention, and of all countries with which the United States has reciprocal copyright relations. All rights, including professional, amateur, motion pictures, recitation, public reading, radio broadcasting, television, video or sound taping, all other forms of mechanical or electronic reproduction, and the rights of translation into foreign languages are strictly reserved.

All inquiries concerning performance rights should be addressed to Samuel French, Inc., 45 West 25th Street, New York, NY 10010, in advance of anticipated production.

Copying from this book in whole or in part is strictly forbidden by law, and the right of performance is not transferable.

Library of Congress Cataloging-in-Publication Data:
Brustein, Robert Sanford, 1927–
   The cherry orchard / in a new adaptation by
   Robert Brustein.
      p.   cm. — (Plays for performance)
   ISBN 1-56663-085-1 (paper). —
   ISBN 1-56663-086-X (cloth)
   1. Gentry—Russia—Drama. I. Chekhov, Anton
   Pavlovich, 1860–1904. Vishnevyĭ sad. English.
II. Title.
III. Series.
PS3552.R845C48   1995
812'.54—dc20   95-11908

INTRODUCTION
by Robert Brustein

The Cherry Orchard was Anton Chekhov's last play, written with great difficulty while he was dying (in 1904) at the age of forty-four. Untimely deaths in literature always make us sad over what might have been, but in Chekhov's case the loss is particularly grievous. Chekhov's dramatic process was one of continuous refinement, not revolutionary formal leaps. Still, by the end of *The Cherry Orchard*, one senses the playwright straining toward new forms, somewhat like Ibsen in *When We Dead Awaken*. Certainly the play looks both forward and backward. A tragicomic eulogy for a passing way of life, it represents some kind of powerful culmination of all Chekhov's dramas up to that time, using the same indirect dramatic method and characters of a similar stripe, type, and class. But it also involves techniques (the strange haunting setting of Act 2, the mysterious broken harp string in Act 1, repeated at the end of Act 4) that give evidence that Chekhov may have been moving in the direction of those dream plays created by Treplev in *The Seagull*.

In short, with *The Cherry Orchard*, which competes in quality with *Three Sisters*, Chekhov had completed his four-play series of group portraits about futilitarians exiled in the provinces, and was ready to move on to different concerns. If only he had lived to do so! The fine mind, discriminating heart, and beautiful soul of Chekhov are among

3

the more compelling reasons that we want "immortal" authors to be truly immortal. Who knows what direction he might have taken had he lived another twenty or thirty years?

It may well be, however, that the soul of Chekhov was reborn a few years later in the body of Samuel Beckett. Certainly Beckett's plays (particularly *Waiting for Godot*) were deeply influenced by Chekhov's notions of double time, his sense of our rapid-tedious progress toward death. Perhaps for that reason, modern Chekhov production has begun to veer away from Stanislavsky realism, which Chekhov himself despised, and light out toward the more impressionistic territory of Beckett landscapes. The American Repertory Theatre production of *The Cherry Orchard*, as directed by Ron Daniels with designs by George Tsypin (sets) and Catherine Zuber (costumes), was, in the tradition of Peter Brooks's *Cherry Orchard* without walls and the electrifying industrial strength *Cherry Orchard* of Andrei Serban, a radical departure from box-set Chekhov. Daniels went so far as to dispense with the traditional birch trees, instead representing the orchard through a series of brightly-lit neon tubes. Tsypin's harsh angular flats, based on the paintings of the Russian artist Malevich, created a perspective that could well have served as a setting for *The Cabinet of Dr. Caligari*.

Within this distended visual surround, however, the acting was distinctly humanistic, particularly in the graceful performance of Claire Bloom as Ranevskaya. For the adaptation, Daniels had requested language that was terse without being colloquial, tough without being hard-boiled, and my task was to provide this modern note without removing the play from its own particular circumstances. Like Jan Kott's view of *Hamlet*, *The*

4

Cherry Orchard is like a sponge in the way it picks up the juices of the environment in which it is produced, like a barometer in the way it records the social-aesthetic pressures of current times. That is why each generation is obliged to reexamine its relationship with Chekhov, in order to record on stage his eternal value for his later contemporaries.

A scene from Act 4 of the American Repertory Theatre production of *The Cherry Orchard*.

CHARACTERS

RANEVSKAYA, LYUBOV ANDREYEVNA, *a landowner*
ANYA, *her daughter, age seventeen*
VARYA, *her adopted daughter, age twenty-seven*
GAYEV, LEONID ANDREYEVICH, *brother of Madame Ranevsky*
LOPAKHIN, YERMOLAI ALEKSEYEVICH, *a merchant*
TROFIMOV, PYOTR SERGEYEVICH, *a student*
SEMYONOV-PISHCHIK, BORIS BOROSOVICH, *a landowner*
CARLOTTA IVANOVNA, *a governess*
EPIHODOV, SEMYON PANTELEYEVICH, *a clerk*
DUNYASHA, *a housemaid*
FIRS, *man-servant, age eighty-seven*
YASHA, *a young man-servant*
TRAMP
Stationmaster, Post Office Official, Guests, Servants, etc.
THE ACTION TAKES PLACE ON MADAME RANEVSKY'S ESTATE

The Cherry Orchard

ACT 1

A room which is still called the nursery. One door leads to Anya's room. Dawn, the sun will soon rise. It is already May, the cherry trees are in blossom, but it is cold in the garden and there is a morning frost. The windows are closed.

Enter Dunyasha with a candle, and Lopakhin with a book in his hand.

LOPAKHIN: Well, thank God the train's in. What time is it?

DUNYASHA: Almost two. *(putting the candle out)* It's light already.

LOPAKHIN: The train's late. At least two hours. *(yawning and stretching)* Look at me. I'm an idiot. I came here expressly to meet them at the station and then went and fell asleep. Dozed off sitting in a chair. What a pain! At least you could have woken me up.

DUNYASHA: I thought you were gone. *(she listens)* I think I hear them driving up.

LOPAKHIN: *(listening)* No; they have to pick up the luggage and things like that. *(a pause)* Lyubov Andreyevna has been out of the country for five years. I wonder what she's like now. What a wonderful woman! Simple, good-natured, kind-hearted. I remember when I was only fifteen,

11

my old father—he kept a shop here in the village then—punched me in the face with his fist and made my nose bleed. We'd come to the courtyard for some reason, I forget why, and he'd been drinking. Lyubov Andreyevna— it seems like yesterday—was still a young girl, and, my, how slender. She made me wash my face, here, in this very room, in the nursery. "Don't cry, little peasant," she said, "it will stop hurting by the time you're married." *(a pause)* "Little peasant!" . . . It's true my father was a peasant, and now look at me in a white vest and orange shoes; like a pig in a pastry shop, as they say. I'm rich now, with lots of money, but when you come to think of it, I'm still a peasant. *(turning over the pages of the book)* Here's this book I was reading and I don't understand a word of it. I just sat here reading and fell asleep.

DUNYASHA: The dogs have been up all night. They know the mistress is coming.

LOPAKHIN: What's the matter with you, Dunyasha? You're all . . .

DUNYASHA: My hands are shaking, I feel like fainting.

LOPAKHIN: You're a soft, spoiled creature, Dunyasha, that's all. You dress like a lady, and your hair's all done up! You ought to be more careful. That's not your place.

(Enter Epihodov with a nosegay. He is dressed in a short jacket and brightly polished boots which squeak noisily. As he comes in he drops the nosegay.)

EPIHODOV: *(picking it up)* The gardener sent this, says you should put it in the dining room. *(handing it to Dunyasha)*

LOPAKHIN: And bring me some kvass.

DUNYASHA: Yes, sir. *(exit Dunyasha)*

EPIHODOV: It's cold this morning, three degrees of frost, and the cherry trees all in bloom. I don't think much of our climate. *(sighing)* It's impossible. Our climate is not auspicious; and I should like to add, with your permission, Yermolai Alekseyevich, that only two days ago I bought myself a new pair of boots, and I venture to assure you that they squeak unbearably. What can I grease them with?

LOPAKHIN: Get out of here. Don't bother me.

EPIHODOV: Every day I'm beset by some new misfortune; but do I complain? No, I'm used to it. I just keep smiling. *(enter Dunyasha, and hands a glass of kvass to Lopakhin)* I must be going. *(he stumbles against a chair, which falls to the ground)* There, you see? *(in a voice of triumph)* If you'll excuse the expression, an accident of a typical nature. It really is amazing! *(exit Epihodov)*

DUNYASHA: I have to tell you, Yermolai Alekseyevich, Epihodov has proposed to me.

LOPAKHIN: Aha!

DUNYASHA: I don't know what to do. He's a very pleasant person, but sometimes I don't know what he's talking about. It's all very nice and full of feeling, but I can't make out what it means. I think I like him, sort of. He loves me passionately. He's a most unfortunate person. Every day something seems to happen to him. They call him "Twenty-two misfortunes." That's his nickname.

LOPAKHIN: *(listening)* There, I really think they're coming!

13

DUNYASHA: They're coming! Oh, what's the matter with me? I'm freezing to death.

LOPAKHIN: Yes, it's really them. Let's go and meet them. Will she still know me, I wonder? It's five years since we last saw each other.

DUNYASHA: I'm going to faint!...I'm going to faint!

(Two carriages are heard driving up to the house. Lopakhin and Dunyasha exeunt quickly. The stage remains empty. A hubbub begins in the neighboring rooms. Firs walks hastily across the stage, leaning on a walking-stick. He has met them at the station. He is wearing old-fashioned livery and a high hat; he mumbles something to himself, but not a word is audible. The noise behind the scenes grows louder and louder. A voice says, "Let's go this way." Enter Madame Ranevsky, Anya, Carlotta, leading a little dog on a chain, all dressed in traveling dresses; Varya in an overcoat, with a kerchief over her head; Gayev, Pishchik, Lopakhin, Dunyasha, carrying a parcel and umbrella, servants with luggage. All cross the stage.)

ANYA: This way, mamma. Do you remember what room this is?

MADAME RANEVSKY: *(joyfully, through her tears)* The nursery.

VARYA: It's so cold. My hands are numb. *(to Madame Ranevsky)* Your two rooms, the white room and the violet room, are just the same as ever, mamma.

MADAME RANEVSKY: My nursery, my dear, beautiful sweet nursery! This is where I used to sleep when I was a little girl. *(crying)* I'm still like a little girl. *(kissing Gayev and Varya and then Gayev again)* Varya hasn't changed a bit, she's still like a nun,

14

and I recognized Dunyasha right away. *(kissing Dunyasha)*

GAYEV: Your train was two hours late. How do you explain that? Is that good management?

CARLOTTA: *(to Pishchik)* My little dog eats nuts.

PISHCHIK: *(astonished)* Is that so? Imagine that! *(exeunt all but Anya and Dunyasha)*

DUNYASHA: You're here at last! *(she takes off Anya's overcoat and hat)*

ANYA: I couldn't sleep for four nights on the trip. I'm so cold.

DUNYASHA: You went away during Lent. There was snow on the ground, but now...! My darling. *(laughing and kissing her)* How I've waited for you, my precious, my joy! Oh, I have something to tell you, I can't wait another minute.

ANYA: *(wearily)* What is it now?

DUNYASHA: Epihodov, the clerk, proposed to me in Easter week.

ANYA: It's always the same old story....*(putting her hair straight)* All my hairpins have fallen out. *(she is very tired, staggering with fatigue)*

DUNYASHA: I don't know what to think of it. He loves me! He loves me so much!

ANYA: *(looking into her bedroom, affectionately)* My own room, my windows, as if I'd never gone away! I'm home again! When I wake up tomorrow morning I'll run out into the garden....Oh, if only I could sleep! I haven't slept the whole trip from Paris, I was so nervous and worried.

DUNYASHA: Pyotr Sergeyevich arrived the day before yesterday.

ANYA: *(joyfully)* Petya?

DUNYASHA: He's asleep in the bathhouse. He's living in there. He's afraid of being in the way, he said. *(looking at her watch)* I'd have waked him, but Varvara Mikhailovna said no. "Be sure you don't wake him," she said.

(enter Varya with a bunch of keys hanging from her waist)

VARYA: Dunyasha, go get some coffee, quick. Mamma wants coffee.

DUNYASHA: In a minute! *(exit Dunyasha)*

VARYA: Well, thank God, you're back. You're home again. *(caressing her)* My little darling is back! My precious pretty one is back!

ANYA: What I had to go through!

VARYA: I can imagine.

ANYA: I left here during Holy Week. It was so cold! Carlotta kept talking the whole way and doing magic tricks. What made you burden me with Carlotta?

VARYA: Well, you couldn't travel alone, my pet. You're only seventeen!

ANYA: When we got to Paris, it was cold there too! Snow was on the ground. My French is terrible. Mamma was on the fifth floor of a big house. I went up to her, and there were a lot of French people there, ladies, an old Catholic priest with a book. It was very uncomfortable and the place smelled of tobacco. I suddenly felt so sorry for mamma, oh, so sorry! I put my arms around her neck and hugged her and couldn't let her go, and mamma kept kissing me and crying.

16

VARYA: *(crying)* Don't talk about it any more, don't talk!

ANYA: She'd sold her villa in Mentone. She had nothing left, absolutely nothing; and I didn't even have a kopek. We barely managed to get home. And mamma won't understand! We get out at a station to have some dinner, and she always orders the most expensive things on the menu and tips each of the waiters a ruble. Carlotta's just the same, and Yasha has to eat exactly what we do. It's just awful! You know, Yasha is mamma's valet now. We brought him back with us.

VARYA: I've seen the rascal.

ANYA: Well, tell me everything! Have you paid the interest on the mortgage?

VARYA: With what?

ANYA: Oh dear! Oh dear!

VARYA: The estate will be sold in August.

ANYA: Oh dear! Oh dear!

LOPAKHIN: *(looking in at the door and mooing like a cow)* Moo-oo! *(he goes away again)*

VARYA: *(weeping, and shaking her fist at the door)* Oh, I'd really like to let him have it!

ANYA: *(embracing Varya softly)* Varya, has he proposed to you yet? *(Varya shakes her head)*

ANYA: But I'm sure he loves you. Why can't you come to an understanding? What are you waiting for?

VARYA: I don't think anything will ever come of it. He's so busy, he doesn't have time for me. He hardly notices me. Damn the man, I can't bear to see him! Everyone talks about our marriage; everyone's always congratulating me, and meanwhile there's nothing to it. It's all a dream. *(changing her tone)* You've got a new brooch like a bee.

ANYA: *(sadly)* Mamma bought it for me. *(going into her room, talking gaily, like a child)* In Paris I went up in a balloon!

VARYA: How happy I am you're back, my little darling! my pretty one! *(Dunyasha has already returned with a coffee pot and begins to prepare the coffee)*

VARYA: *(standing by the door)* I take care of the house all day, and I'm always thinking. What are we going to do? If only we could marry you off to some rich man, I could relax a little. I'd go on a retreat, and then go to Kiev, to Moscow. I'd wander from one holy place to another, always moving, always moving. What bliss!

ANYA: The birds are singing in the orchard. What time is it now?

VARYA: Must be after two. Time to go to bed, my darling. *(following Anya into her room)* What bliss! *(enter Yasha with a shawl and a traveling bag)*

YASHA: *(crossing the stage, delicately)* May I pass through here, mademoiselle?

DUNYASHA: I'd hardly know you, Yasha. You really changed abroad!

YASHA: Hmm! and who are you, pray?

DUNYASHA: When you went away, I was only that high *(indicating with her hand)*. I'm Dunyasha, Fyodor's daughter. Don't you remember me?

18

YASHA: Hmm! You're some little peach! *(He looks round cautiously, then embraces her. She screams and drops a saucer. Exit Yasha hastily.)*

VARYA: *(in the doorway, crossly)* What was that about?

DUNYASHA: *(crying)* I broke a saucer.

VARYA: Well, that brings luck. *(enter Anya from her room)*

ANYA: We must let mamma know that Petya's here.

VARYA: I left orders not to wake him.

ANYA: *(thoughtfully)* It's six years since papa died. A month later poor little Grisha drowned in the river, only seven years old, my pretty little brother! It was too much for mamma, so she ran away, ran away without looking back. *(shuddering)* I understand her so well, if only she knew! *(a pause)* And Petya Trofimov was Grisha's tutor; he might remind her.

(enter Firs in long coat and white waistcoat)

FIRS: *(going over to the coffee pot, anxiously)* My mistress will take her coffee here. *(putting on white gloves)* Is the coffee ready? *(sternly, to Dunyasha)* Girl, where's the cream?

DUNYASHA: Oh dear! oh dear! *(exit Dunyasha hastily)*

FIRS: *(bustling about the coffee pot)* Ech, you ... good for nothing! *(mumbling to himself)* She's come back from Paris. The master went to Paris once ... horses all the way. *(laughing)*

VARYA: What is it, Firs?

FIRS: I beg your pardon? *(joyfully)* My mistress has come home; at last I've seen her. Now I'm ready to die. *(He cries with joy. Enter Madame Ranevsky,*

Lopakhin, Gayev, and Pishchik; Pishchik in Russian breeches and coat of fine cloth. Gayev as he enters makes gestures as if playing billiards.)

MADAME RANEVSKY: How does it go? Let me see. "Red in the corner pocket."

GAYEV: That's it, or in off the white. When we were children, Lyuba, we used to sleep here together in two little cots, and now I'm fifty-one, and I can't believe it.

LOPAKHIN: Yes; time, they say, flies.

GAYEV: What's that?

LOPAKHIN: Time flies, they say.

GAYEV: What a smell of garlic!

ANYA: I am going to bed. Good night, mamma. *(kissing her mother)*

MADAME RANEVSKY: My sweet little girl! *(kissing her hands)* Aren't you glad you're home? I can't believe it.

ANYA: Good night, uncle.

GAYEV: *(kissing her face and hands)* God bless you, little Anya. You're just like your mother. *(to Madame Ranevsky)* You were just like her at that age, Lyuba.

(Anya shakes hands with Lopakhin and Pishchik, and exits, shutting her bedroom door behind her)

MADAME RANEVSKY: She's totally exhausted.

PISHCHIK: It must have been a very long trip.

VARYA: *(to Lopakhin and Pishchik)* Well, gentlemen, it's almost three o'clock. Time to say goodbye.

MADAME RANEVSKY: *(laughing)* You haven't changed a bit, Varya! *(drawing her to herself and kissing her)* I'll just finish my coffee, then we'll all go. *(Firs puts a footstool under her feet)* Thank you, friend. I need my coffee. I drink it day and night. Thank you, you dear old man. *(kissing Firs)*

VARYA: I'll go see if they've got all the luggage. *(exit Varya)*

MADAME RANEVSKY: Is it really me sitting here? *(laughing)* I want to dance and clap my hands. *(pausing and covering her face)* I think I must be dreaming! God knows I love my country. I love it deeply. I couldn't see out the train window, I was crying so much. *(crying)* But...I must drink my coffee. Thank you, Firs; thank you, you dear old man. I'm so glad to find you still alive.

FIRS: The day before yesterday.

GAYEV: He's a little deaf.

LOPAKHIN: I have to go to Kharkov on the five-o'clock train. Such a bother! I wanted to stay and look at you and talk to you. You're as wonderful as ever.

PISHCHIK: *(sighing heavily)* Even more beautiful, and dressed like a Parisian....You could blow me down!

LOPAKHIN: Your brother, Leonid Andreyevich, says I'm an upstart, a money-grubber. He can say whatever he likes. I don't care a bit. I just want you to believe in me like in the old days. I just want your wonderful, tender eyes to look at me like they did then. Good God in heaven! My father was one of your father's serfs, and your grandfather's serf before that, but you, you did so much for me in the old days that I've forgotten all that. I love you like a sister—more than a sister.

MADAME RANEVSKY: I can't sit still! I can't! *(jumping up and walking about in great agitation)* I can't bear it, I'm so happy. Yes, laugh at me! I know I'm silly! *(kissing the bookcase)* My adorable bookcase! *(caressing the table)* My sweet little table!

GAYEV: Nurse died while you were away.

MADAME RANEVSKY: *(sitting down and drinking coffee)* Yes, heaven rest her soul. You wrote me about that.

GAYEV: And Anastasy is dead. Cross-eyed Petrushka has left us and works in the town at the police inspector's office. *(takes a box of caramels from his pocket and begins to eat them)*

PISHCHIK: My daughter Dashenka sends her compliments.

LOPAKHIN: I want to say something cheering and pleasant to you. *(looking at his watch)* But I'm off; there's no time to talk. Well, yes, I'll say two or three words. You know that your cherry orchard is up for sale to pay the mortgage. The auction is fixed for the twenty-second of August. But don't be nervous, dear lady; sleep peacefully, there's a way to save it. Here's my plan. Listen carefully. Your estate is only fifteen miles from town; the railway runs near it; and if you cut up the cherry orchard and the land along the river into building lots and rent it out for villas, you could make at least twenty-five thousand rubles a year.

GAYEV: What nonsense are you talking?

MADAME RANEVSKY: I don't quite understand you, Yermolai Alekseyevich.

LOPAKHIN: The summer tenants will pay you at least twenty-five rubles a year for every three acres, and if you advertise now, I'll bet you anything that by autumn you won't have a square foot of land left. All the plots will be snapped up. Congratulations. You're saved. You've got a first-class site, with a good deep river. Only of course you'll have to clear it all, pull down all the old buildings. This house, too, which isn't good for anything any more. You'll have to cut down the cherry orchard....

MADAME RANEVSKY: Cut down the cherry orchard! Excuse me, dear friend, but you don't know what you're talking about. If there is one thing interesting, in fact remarkable, in this whole province, it's our cherry orchard.

LOPAKHIN: The only remarkable thing about your cherry orchard is that it's a very big one. It only bears cherries once every two years, and then you don't know what to do with the fruit. Nobody buys it.

GAYEV: Our cherry orchard is mentioned in Andreyevsky's *Encyclopaedia*.

LOPAKHIN: *(looking at his watch)* Look, if we don't move fast and take the right steps, on the twenty-second of August your cherry orchard and the whole property will be sold by auction. Come on, make up your minds! There's no other way, I swear it—absolutely none.

FIRS: In the old days, forty or fifty years ago, they used to dry the cherries and soak them and pickle them, and make jam out of them. And the dried cherries...

GAYEV: Shut up, Firs.

FIRS: The dried cherries were sent in wagons to Moscow and Kharkov. That brought in pots of money! The dried cherries were soft and juicy and sweet and sweet-smelling then. They knew how to do it in those days.

MADAME RANEVSKY: And not now?

FIRS: They've forgotten. Nobody knows the recipe any more.

PISHCHIK: *(to Madame Ranevsky)* What was it like in Paris? Did you eat frogs there?

MADAME RANEVSKY: Crocodiles.

PISHCHIK: Really! Imagine that!

LOPAKHIN: Until a little while ago there were only gentlefolks and peasants in the country; but now these summer visitors are coming. All the towns, even the smallest ones, are surrounded by villas now. In another twenty years you can be sure these people will be everywhere. Now the summer visitor only sits and drinks tea on his veranda, but soon he'll probably start working his three acres of land, and then your old cherry orchard will become fruitful, rich, and bountiful. . . .

GAYEV: *(angry)* What nonsense!

(enter Varya and Yasha)

VARYA: *(taking out a key and noisily unlocking an old-fashioned bookcase)* There are two telegrams for you, mamma. Here they are.

MADAME RANEVSKY: *(tearing them up without reading them)* They're from Paris. Paris is over.

GAYEV: Do you know how old this bookcase is, Lyuba? A week ago I pulled out the bottom drawer and saw a date burnt in it. That cupboard was made exactly a hundred years ago. What do you think of that, eh? We should have celebrated its jubilee. It may be only an inanimate object, but still that bookcase is historic.

PISHCHIK: *(astonished)* A hundred years? Well, imagine that!

GAYEV: *(touching the cupboard)* Yes, it's really a wonder.... Beloved and venerable cupboard; hail to thee, who for more than a hundred years has served the noble ideals of justice and virtue. In all these hundred years, your silent call to profitable labor has never weakened. *(crying)* You have upheld the faith and courage of succeeding generations of humanity in a better future dedicated to ideals of virtue and social consciousness. *(a pause)*

LOPAKHIN: Yes....

MADAME RANEVSKY: You haven't changed a bit, Leonid.

GAYEV: *(embarrassed)* Red in the corner pocket, chipped off the blue!

LOPAKHIN: *(looking at his watch)* Well, I've got to go.

YASHA: *(handing a box to Madame Ranevsky)* Perhaps you're ready for your pills now?

PISHCHIK: You shouldn't take medicine, dear lady. It doesn't help either way. Give them to me, my friend. *(he empties all the pills into the palm of his hand, blows on them, puts them in his mouth, and swallows them down with a glass of kvass)* There!

MADAME RANEVSKY: *(alarmed)* Have you gone out of your mind?

25

PISHCHIK: I've taken all the pills.

LOPAKHIN: What a glutton! *(everyone laughs)*

FIRS: *(mumbling)* He was here in Easter week and finished off a gallon of pickled cucumbers. *(mutters)*

MADAME RANEVSKY: What's he talking about?

VARYA: He's been muttering like that for the last three years. We're used to it.

YASHA: Advancing age.

(Carlotta crosses in a white frock, very thin, tightly laced, with a lorgnette at her waist)

LOPAKHIN: Excuse me, Carlotta Ivanovna, I haven't said hello to you yet. *(he prepares to kiss her hand)*

CARLOTTA: *(drawing her hand away)* If I let you kiss my hand, you'll want to kiss my elbow next, and then my shoulder.

LOPAKHIN: I'm completely out of luck today. *(all laugh)* Carlotta Ivanovna, show us a magic trick.

MADAME RANEVSKY: Carlotta, please show us a magic trick.

CARLOTTA: No, thanks. I'm going to bed. *(she exits)*

LOPAKHIN: We'll be together again in three weeks. *(kissing Madame Ranevsky's hand)* Goodbye till then. I have to go. *(to Gayev)* Farewell. *(kissing Pishchik)* See you soon. *(shaking hands with Varya, then with Firs and Yasha)* I don't want to go. *(to Madame Ranevsky)* Let me know if you decide about the villas, and I'll put up fifty thousand rubles right away, as a loan. Think about it seriously.

VARYA: *(angrily)* Leave, for heaven's sake!

LOPAKHIN: I'm going, I'm going. *(he exits)*

GAYEV: Upstart!...However, *pardon*. Varya's going to marry him; he's Varya's fiancé.

VARYA: You talk too much, uncle.

MADAME RANEVSKY: But, Varya, I would be very happy. He's a good man.

PISHCHIK: No doubt about it...a very worthy individual. My Dashenka, she says...she says...lots of things. *(snoring and waking up again at once)* By the way, dear lady, can you lend me two hundred forty rubles? I have to pay the interest on my mortgage tomorrow.

VARYA: *(alarmed)* Impossible! Impossible!

MADAME RANEVSKY: I really have no money.

PISHCHIK: It'll turn up. *(laughing)* I never lose hope. Last time I thought, "Hey, I'm really finished. This time I'm really ruined," when, presto, they put a railroad through my land and paid me compensation. And something will turn up again, if not today, then tomorrow. Dashenka may win two hundred thousand. She bought a lottery ticket.

MADAME RANEVSKY: I've finished my coffee. Let's go to bed.

FIRS: *(brushing Gayev's clothes, admonishingly)* You put on the wrong pair of trousers again. What am I going to do with you?

VARYA: *(softly)* Anya's asleep. *(she opens the window quietly)* The sun's up already; it's warming up. Look, mamma, how lovely the trees are. My heavens, what sweet air! The starlings are singing!

27

GAYEV: *(opening the other window)* The orchard is all white. Do you remember it, Lyuba? That long avenue running straight on, straight on, like a ribbon between the trees? On moonlight nights it shines like silver. Do you remember, Lyuba? You haven't forgotten?

MADAME RANEVSKY: *(looking out into the garden)* Oh, my childhood, my innocent childhood! I used to sleep in this nursery. I looked out from here into the garden. I woke up happy every morning; and the orchard is just the same as in the old days; nothing has changed. *(laughing with joy)* All white, all white! Oh, my cherry orchard! After the dark stormy autumn and the winter frosts you are young again and full of happiness; the heavenly angels have never abandoned you. Oh, if only I could be free of the stone that weighs me down! If only I could forget my past!

GAYEV: Yes, and now the orchard will be sold to pay our debts, which seems impossible. . . .

MADAME RANEVSKY: Look! It's mamma walking in the orchard . . . in a white dress! *(laughing with joy)* there she is!

GAYEV: Where?

VARYA: Mamma, don't!

MADAME RANEVSKY: It's no one really. Just my imagination. Down there on the right where the path turns toward the summer house; there's a white tree leaning over that looks like a woman. *(enter Trofimov in a shabby student uniform and spectacles)* What a gorgeous orchard, with its white masses of blossom under the blue sky!

TROFIMOV: Lyubov Andreyevna! *(she looks round at him)* I'll just say hello and then go away. *(kissing*

28

her hand eagerly) They told me to wait until morning, but I didn't have the patience.

(Madame Ranevsky looks at him in astonishment)

VARYA: *(crying)* This is Petya Trofimov.

TROFIMOV: Petya Trofimov. I was Grisha's tutor. Have I changed so much?

(Madame Ranevsky embraces him and cries softly)

GAYEV: *(in confusion)* Come, come, that's enough, Lyuba!

VARYA: *(crying)* I told you to wait until tomorrow, Petya.

MADAME RANEVSKY: My little Grisha! My little boy! Grisha...my child....

VARYA: It can't be helped, mamma. It was God's will.

TROFIMOV: *(gently, crying)* There, there!

MADAME RANEVSKY: *(crying)* My boy was drowned. My little boy was drowned. Why? What was the sense of that, dear Petya? *(in a softer voice)* Anya's asleep in there, and I'm talking too loud, making this noise....But Petya, why have you grown so ugly? Why have you grown so old?

TROFIMOV: A woman on the train the other day called me a mangy-looking gentleman.

MADAME RANEVSKY: You were such a boy then, a sweet little student, and now your hair's going thin and you wear glasses. Are you really still a student? *(going toward the door)*

TROFIMOV: Yes, I expect I'll always be a student.

MADAME RANEVSKY: *(kissing her brother and then Varya)* Well, go to bed. You've gotten older too, Leonid.

PISHCHIK: *(following her)* Yes, yes, it's time for bed. Ooof, my gout! I'll spend the night here. Don't forget, Lyubov Andreyevna, my angel, if you could, tomorrow morning... two hundred forty rubles.

GAYEV: The same old story.

PISHCHIK: Two hundred forty rubles... to pay the interest on my mortgage.

MADAME RANEVSKY: My dear friend, I have no money.

PISHCHIK: I'll pay it back, dear lady. It's really nothing.

MADAME RANEVSKY: Oh well, Leonid will give it to you. Give him the money, Leonid.

GAYEV: *(ironical)* I'll give it to him all right! Don't hold your breath!

MADAME RANEVSKY: We have no choice.... He needs it. He'll pay it back.

(Exeunt Madame Ranevksy, Trofimov, Pishchik, and Firs. Gayev, Varya, and Yasha remain.)

GAYEV: My sister hasn't lost her habit of throwing money away. *(to Yasha)* Go away, my dear fellow! You smell of the henhouse.

YASHA: *(laughing)* And you, Leonid Andreyevich, haven't changed a bit.

GAYEV: What's that? *(to Varya)* What did he say?

VARYA: *(to Yasha)* Your mother's here from the village. She's been waiting for you since yesterday in the servants' quarters. She's anxious to see you.

YASHA: She's a pain in the neck!

VARYA: You're a vile, unnatural son!

YASHA: Well, what am I going to do with her? She could have come tomorrow. *(exit Yasha)*

VARYA: Mamma's the same as ever; she hasn't changed at all. If she had her way, she'd give away everything.

GAYEV: Yes. *(a pause)* If people propose a lot of cures for an illness, that means the illness is incurable. I think and I think, I rack my brains. I have a lot of schemes, a lot, and that really means that none will work. How nice it would be if someone left us a fortune! How nice it would be if Anya could marry a very rich man! How nice it would be if I went to Yaroslav and got the money from my aunt, the Countess. My aunt is very, very rich, you know.

VARYA: *(crying softly)* If only God would help us!

GAYEV: Stop blubbering! My aunt is very rich, but she doesn't like us. First, my sister married a lawyer instead of an aristocrat. *(Anya appears in the doorway)* She married a man from another class, and there's no sense pretending she's led a virtuous life. She's a dear, kind, pleasant creature, and I love her very much, but however you excuse it, there's no blinking the fact she's a sinful woman. You see it in her slightest gesture.

VARYA: *(whispering)* Anya's in the doorway!

GAYEV: What did you say? *(a pause)* Strange, but something got into my right eye. I can't see through it very well. Last Thursday when I was down at the district court...*(Anya comes down)*

VARYA: Why aren't you asleep, Anya?

ANYA: I can't sleep.

GAYEV: My little pet! *(kissing Anya's hands and face)* My little girl! *(crying)* You're not my niece; you're my angel, my everything. Believe me, believe me....

ANYA: I do believe you, uncle. Everyone loves you, everyone respects you. But dear, dear uncle, you have to watch your mouth, you have to try to keep quiet. What were you saying just now about mamma, your own sister? Why would you say such a thing?

GAYEV: Yes, yes. *(covering his face with her hand)* You're absolutely right. That was awful! My God, my God, save me from myself! And a little while ago I delivered a speech to the bookcase. What a stupid thing to do! The minute I said it, I knew it was stupid.

VARYA: Yes, uncle, you really ought to keep quiet. Don't talk; that's the best thing.

ANYA: If you could just stop talking, you'd be happier too!

GAYEV: I will! I will! *(kissing Anya's and Varya's hands)* I'll keep my mouth shut. But this is about business. Last Thursday, when I was down at the district court, a lot of us were there and we began to talk about this and that, about one thing and another, and it looks like I could arrange a loan on an I.O.U. to pay the interest to the bank.

VARYA: If only God would help us!

GAYEV: I'll go down Tuesday and look into it again. *(to Varya)* Don't blubber! *(to Anya)* Your mamma will have a talk with Lopakhin. He can't possibly refuse her. And as soon as you're rested you'll go see your great aunt, the Countess, at Yaroslav. We'll move in on the problem from three different directions, and we'll turn the trick. The interest will be paid, I'm certain of it. *(taking a caramel)* I swear it on my honor, or whatever, that the estate will not be sold. *(excitedly)* I swear it on my future happiness! Here's my hand on it. Call me a base, vile man if I ever let it go to auction. I swear it on my soul!

ANYA: *(calm again and happy)* How good you are, uncle, and how clever! *(embraces him)* I'm at peace again. Completely at peace! I'm happy!

(enter Firs)

FIRS: *(reproachfully)* Leonid Andreyevich, have you no fear of God? When are you going to bed?

GAYEV: I'm going, I'm going. You can go, Firs. I'll undress myself tonight. Come, children, nighty-night! Details tomorrow, but now let's go to bed. *(kissing Anya and Varya)* I'm a good liberal, a man of the eighties. People say bad things about the eighties, but I think I can say I've suffered for my convictions in my time. It's not an accident that the peasants love me. We have to get to know the peasants; we have to learn from what...

ANYA: You're at it again, uncle!

VARYA: Uncle, please hold your tongue!

FIRS: *(angrily)* Leonid Andreyevich!

GAYEV: I'm coming, I'm coming. Go to bed. Off two cushions in the center pocket! I'm starting a new life!...*(exit, with Firs hobbling after him)*

ANYA: My mind is easy now. I don't want to go to Yaroslav; I don't like my great aunt; but my mind is easy, thanks to Uncle Leonid. *(she sits down)*

VARYA: We have to go to bed. I'm going. Something unpleasant happened while you were gone. You know, nobody lives in the old servants' quarters except the old servants, Efhimyushka, Polya, Yevstigney, and old Karp. Well, they started letting all kinds of strange types spend the night there with them. I didn't say a word. But then I heard they were saying I had given orders they could only eat pease pudding. Out of stinginess, you know. It was all Yevstigney's doing. All right, I said to myself, just you wait. So I sent for Yevstigney. *(yawning)* And he comes. Now then, Yevstigney, you old imbecile, I said, how dare you....*(looking at Anya)* Anya! Anitchka! *(a pause)* Fast asleep. *(taking Anya's arm)* Come to bed. Come along. *(leading her away)* Sleep on, my little one! Come along, come along! *(They go toward Anya's room. In the distance beyond the orchard, a shepherd plays his pipe. Trofimov crosses the stage and, seeing Varya and Anya, stops.)* Ssh, she's asleep, my darling is asleep! Come along, my sweet.

ANYA: *(drowsily)* I'm so tired! Listen to those bells! Uncle, dear uncle! Mamma! Uncle!

VARYA: Come along, my dearest! Come along. *(exeunt Varya and Anya to the bedroom)*

TROFIMOV: *(with emotion)* My sunshine! My spring!

ACT 2

In the open fields; an old crooked half-ruined shrine. Near it a well; big stones, apparently old tombstones; an old bench. Road to the estate beyond. On one side rise dark poplar trees. Beyond them begins the cherry orchard. In the distance a row of telegraph poles, and, far away on the horizon, the dim outlines of a big town, visible only in clear weather. It is near sunset.

Carlotta, Yasha, and Dunyasha sit on the bench. Epihodov stands by them and plays on a guitar; they meditate. Carlotta wears an old peaked cap. She has taken a gun from off her shoulders and is fixing the buckle of the strap.

CARLOTTA: *(thoughtfully)* I don't have a valid passport. I don't know how old I am, so I always feel quite young. When I was a little girl my father and mother used to travel to country fairs, giving performances. Good ones, too. I used to do the *salto mortale* and other kinds of tricks. When papa and mamma died, an old German lady took me in and got me educated. When I grew up, I became a governess. But where I come from and who I am, I haven't the slightest idea. Who my parents were—I doubt if they were married—I don't know. *(taking a cucumber from her pocket and beginning to eat)* I know nothing about it. *(a pause)* I really want to talk, and there's no one to talk to, no friends or relations.

EPIHODOV: *(playing on the guitar and singing)* "Who cares about this noisy world? Who cares for friends or foes?" How sweet it is to play upon a mandolin!

DUNYASHA: That's not a mandolin, it's a guitar. *(she looks at herself in a hand mirror and powders her face)*

EPIHODOV: For a man mad with love, it's a mandolin. *(singing)*
"If only my heart were warmed
By the glow of requited love." *(Yasha joins in)*

CARLOTTA: What rotten singing! Foo! Like the howling of jackals!

DUNYASHA: *(to Yasha)* It must be wonderful to live abroad!

YASHA: You're right, it is. *(he yawns and lights a cigar)*

EPIHODOV: That makes absolute sense. Everything abroad has achieved a certain culmination.

YASHA: You're right.

EPIHODOV: I am a cultivated man; I have pored over a variety of extraordinary books, but I cannot determine the options of my tendencies. Do I want to live or shoot myself, so to speak? So as to be ready for all contingencies, I always carry a revolver in my pocket. Here it is. *(showing revolver)*

CARLOTTA: That's it. I'm off. *(slinging the rifle over her shoulder)* You're a very clever fellow, Epihodov, and very terrifying. Women must fall all over you. Brrr! *(going)* These clever people are all so stupid. I have no one to talk to. I am alone, always alone. I have no friends or relations, and who I am, or why I exist, is a total mystery to me. *(exit slowly)*

EPIHODOV: To speak precisely, apart from other matters, I must affirm that destiny treats me abominably, as a storm might treat a little boat. If I misconceive things, why, for example, when I woke up this morning, did I perceive sitting on my chest a spider of extravagant dimensions? Like that! *(indicating with both hands)* And if I go to take a swig of kvass, I invariably find something of the most indelicate character in the jug, like a cockroach. *(a pause)* Have you read Buckle? *(a pause)* *(to Dunyasha)* May I trouble you, Avdotya Fyodorovna, with a few words.

DUNYASHA: Talk away.

EPIHODOV: I should prefer a *tête-à-tête*. *(sighing)*

DUNYASHA: *(confused)* Very well, but first please get me my cloak. It's near the cupboard. It's rather damp here.

EPIHODOV: Very well, I will go and fetch it. Now I know what to do with my revolver. *(takes his guitar and exits, playing)*

YASHA: Twenty-two misfortunes! Between you and me, he's a real dope. *(yawning)*

DUNYASHA: I hope, pray God, he doesn't shoot himself! *(a pause)* I've gotten so nervous, I am always in a twitter. I was only a little girl when they took me into the house, so I don't like common behavior, and my hands are as white as white, like a lady's. I've grown so refined, so delicate and genteel, I'm afraid of everything. I'm always frightened. And if you deceive me, Yasha, my nerves will never stand it.

YASHA: *(kissing her)* You're a real peach! Of course a girl ought to watch her morals. There's nothing

37

I hate so much as a girl who doesn't watch her morals.

DUNYASHA: I've fallen dreadfully in love with you, Yasha. You're so cultured; you can talk about anything! *(a pause)*

YASHA: *(yawning)* Yes, that's true. . . . This is the way I look at it: if a girl falls in love with someone, that means she's immoral. *(a pause)* It's really nice to smoke a cigar in the open air. *(listening)* Someone's coming. It's the mistress and the others. . . . *(Dunyasha embraces him hastily)* Go to the house like you'd just had a swim. Take this path or else they'll see you and think you've been with me. I can't stand that kind of thing.

DUNYASHA: *(coughing softly)* Your cigar has given me a headache.

(Exit Dunyasha. Yasha remains sitting by the shrine. Enter Madame Ranevsky, Gayev, and Lopakhin.)

LOPAKHIN: You've got to make your minds up once and for all. Time won't wait. It's a very simple question. Are you going to use the land for villas or not? Just one word; yes or no? Just one word!

MADAME RANEVSKY: Who's been smoking those horrible cigars here? *(she sits down)*

GAYEV: It's so convenient now that they've built that railroad. *(sitting)* We've been able to have lunch in town and get back again. Cannon off the red! I want to go to the house and play a game.

MADAME RANEVSKY: Later.

LOPAKHIN: Just one word—yes or no! *(entreatingly)* Come on, answer the question!

GAYEV: *(yawning)* How's that?

MADAME RANEVSKY: *(looking into her purse)* Yesterday I had lots of money, but there's hardly any left now. Poor Varya tries to save by feeding us milk soup, the old people in the kitchen get nothing but pease pudding, and yet I go on squandering shamelessly.... *(dropping her purse and scattering gold coins; vexed)* Look, I've dropped everything!

YASHA: Permit me, I'll pick it up. *(collecting the coins)*

MADAME RANEVSKY: Yes, please do, Yasha! Why did I go into town for lunch? That restaurant of yours is horrid, with that wretched band and tablecloths smelling of soap. Why do you drink so much, Leonid? And eat so much? Why do you talk so much? You talked too much at the restaurant again today, and so unsuitably, about the seventies, and the decadents. And to whom? Imagine talking about the decadents to waiters!

LOPAKHIN: That's true.

GAYEV: *(with a gesture)* I'm incorrigible, that's plain. *(irritably to Yasha)* Why do you keep running around in front of me?

YASHA: *(laughing)* I can't listen to your voice without laughing.

GAYEV: *(to Madame Ranevsky)* It's him or me...

MADAME RANEVSKY: Go away, Yasha; run along.

YASHA: *(handing Madame Ranevsky her purse)* I'll go right away. *(restraining his laughter with difficulty)* This very second. *(he exits)*

LOPAKHIN: Deriganov, the millionaire, would like to buy your estate. They say he's coming to the auction in person.

MADAME RANEVSKY: Where did you hear that?

LOPAKHIN: They told me in town.

GAYEV: Our aunt at Yaroslav has promised to send something; but I don't know when, or how much.

LOPAKHIN: How much? A hundred thousand? Two hundred?

MADAME RANEVSKY: Oh, come.... Ten or fifteen thousand at the most.

LOPAKHIN: Excuse me, but in all my life I have never met anyone as frivolous as you two, such reckless and impractical people! I tell you in plain Russian that your estate is going to be sold, and you don't understand a word I say.

MADAME RANEVSKY: Well, what should we do? Tell us what to do.

LOPAKHIN: I tell you every day. Every day I say the same thing over and over. You must rent out the cherry orchard and the rest of the estate for villas. At once, right this second. The auction is coming up very soon! Try and understand. As soon as you make up your mind to build villas, you'll have all the money you want, and you're saved.

MADAME RANEVSKY: Villas and summer residents, oh, please, ... It's so vulgar!

GAYEV: I agree with you completely.

LOPAKHIN: I'm going to cry, or scream, or faint. I can't stand it! You're driving me mad. *(to Gayev)* You're just an old woman.

GAYEV: How's that?

LOPAKHIN: You're an old woman! *(going)*

MADAME RANEVSKY: *(frightened)* No, don't go. Stay here, my dear! Perhaps we'll think of something else.

LOPAKHIN: What's the good of thinking!

MADAME RANEVSKY: Please don't go. At least it's cheerful with you here. *(a pause)* I keep expecting something to happen, like the house was going to fall down on us.

GAYEV: *(in deep dejection)* Off the cushion in the corner; double into the center pocket....

MADAME RANEVSKY: We have been very, very sinful!

LOPAKHIN: You! What sins have you committed?

GAYEV: *(eating candy)* They say I've eaten all my substance up in caramels. *(laughing)*

MADAME RANEVSKY: Oh, the sins that I've committed.... I've always thrown away money recklessly like a mad person. I married a man who made nothing but debts. He drank himself to death on champagne, he was a terrible drinker. To add to my misery I fell in love and went off with another man; and immediately—this was my first punishment—came the blow... here, in this river... my little boy was drowned; and I went abroad, right away, never to return, never again to see this river.... I shut my eyes and ran, like a mad thing, and he came after me, pitiless and cruel. I bought a villa in Mentone, because he got sick there, and for three years I had no rest, day or night. His illness wore me out, dried up my soul. And last year, when my villa was sold to pay off my debts, I went to Paris, and there he came to rob me of everything, then left me

for another woman, and I tried to poison my-self....It was all so stupid, so humiliating....
Then suddenly I felt a great longing for Russia, for my own country, for my little girl....*(wiping away her tears)* Lord, Lord, be merciful to me; forgive my sins! Don't punish me any more! *(taking a telegram from her pocket)* This came today from Paris....He begs me to forgive him, implores me to take him back....*(tearing up the telegram)* Do I hear music somewhere? *(listening)*

GAYEV: That's our famous Jewish orchestra. You remember? Four fiddles, a flute, and a double bass.

MADAME RANEVSKY: Is that still around? We ought to invite them some evening, and have a dance.

LOPAKHIN: *(listening)* I don't hear anything. *(singing softly)* "The Germans for a fee will turn a Russian into a Frenchman." *(laughing)* I saw a very funny play at the theatre last night; awfully funny!

MADAME RANEVSKY: It probably wasn't funny at all. You people shouldn't look at plays; you should look at yourselves, to see what grey lives you lead. And how much nonsense you talk.

LOPAKHIN: True enough. To be honest, we live a stupid life. *(a pause)* My father was a peasant, a moron. He understood nothing; he taught me nothing; all he did was beat me with his stick when he got drunk. As it turns out, I'm just as big an idiot as he was. I never studied; my handwriting's rotten; I write so badly I'm ashamed before people; like a pig.

MADAME RANEVSKY: You ought to get married.

LOPAKHIN: Yes, that's true.

42

MADAME RANEVSKY: You ought to marry Varya. She's a good girl.

LOPAKHIN: Yes.

MADAME RANEVSKY: She's a good-natured creature. She works hard, and what's most important, she loves you. You've been fond of her for a long time.

LOPAKHIN: Well, why not? I'm perfectly willing. She's a very nice girl. *(a pause)*

GAYEV: They've offered me a place in a bank. Six thousand rubles a year. Did you hear?

MADAME RANEVSKY: You in a bank! Stay where you are. *(enter Firs, carrying an overcoat)*

FIRS: *(to Gayev)* Please put this on, sir; it's getting damp.

GAYEV: *(putting on the coat)* You're a pain in the neck, Firs!

FIRS: What am I to do about you.... You went off this morning without telling me. *(examining his clothes)*

MADAME RANEVSKY: You've gotten so old, Firs!

FIRS: What's that?

LOPAKHIN: She says you've gotten old!

FIRS: I've been alive a long time. Your father wasn't even born yet when they arranged my marriage. *(laughing)* I was already the head servant when the emancipation came. But I refused to be set free; I stayed with the master. *(a pause)* I remember how happy everybody was, but what they were happy about, no one knows.

LOPAKHIN: That was a fine time. Lots of flogging.

43

FIRS: *(mishearing him)* I should think so! The peasants knew their place, and the masters knew theirs, but now it's all so mixed up, you can't make it out.

GAYEV: Shut up, Firs. I have to go to town again tomorrow. They've promised to introduce me to a general who might lend us money.

LOPAKHIN: That won't work. It won't even pay the interest, you can count on that.

MADAME RANEVSKY: *(to Lopakhin)* He's just talking nonsense. There isn't any general.

(enter Trofimov, Anya, and Varya)

GAYEV: Here come our girls.

ANYA: There's mamma.

MADAME RANEVSKY: *(tenderly)* Come along, come along...my little darlings....*(embracing Anya and Varya)* If you only knew how much I love you both! Sit next to me...there, like that. *(everyone sits)*

LOPAKHIN: Our perpetual student is always hanging around the ladies.

TROFIMOV: That's none of your business.

LOPAKHIN: He'll soon be fifty and he's still a student.

TROFIMOV: Enough of your stupid jokes!

LOPAKHIN: Why are you losing your temper, you strange fellow?

TROFIMOV: Just leave me alone.

LOPAKHIN: *(laughing)* I'd like to know what you really think of me?

44

TROFIMOV: What I really think of you, Yermolai Alekseyevich, is this. You're a rich man. You'll soon be a millionaire. But just as we need predatory animals to maintain the balance of nature, so we need you. *(all laugh)*

VARYA: Teach us about the planets instead, Petya.

MADAME RANEVSKY: No. Let's continue with the conversation we were having yesterday.

TROFIMOV: Remind me what it was about.

GAYEV: It was about pride.

TROFIMOV: We talked a lot yesterday, but we didn't come to any conclusions. There is something mystical about pride in the sense you use the word. From your point of view, that may be right, but if we look at it simply, what's the use of pride? Is there any purpose to it, when man is so imperfectly created, when the vast majority is so coarse and stupid, so deeply unhappy? We must give up vanity and self-glorification. We must work, and nothing else.

GAYEV: We'll still die, all the same.

TROFIMOV: Who knows? And what does it mean, to die? Perhaps man has a hundred senses, and when he dies only the five senses we know die with him, while the remaining ninety-five still go on living.

MADAME RANEVSKY: You're so clever, Petya.

LOPAKHIN: *(ironically)* A genius!

TROFIMOV: Humankind marches forward, perfecting itself. Everything that is beyond us now will one day be familiar and attainable. But we must work, we must use all our strength to help those who seek for truth. Only a few people work in Russia now. The great majority of the educated people I know seek nothing, do nothing, and are unfit for work of any kind. They call themselves "intellectuals," but they patronize their servants and treat the peasants like animals. They learn nothing, read no serious books, do nothing useful, talk only about science, and understand virtually nothing about art. They are all very serious; look very solemn; discuss only burning issues and theorize incessantly. But the rest of us, the vast majority, 99 percent, live like savages, cursing and punching people at the slightest provocation. We eat like pigs and sleep crowded together in filth and foul air, bedbugs everywhere, stench and damp and moral deterioration.... It's obvious that all our clever debates are only meant to distract our attention and that of other people. Show me those day nurseries they're all talking about; or those reading rooms. They only talk of these things in novels; they don't really exist at all. Nothing exists but filth, vulgarity, and Asiatic sloth. I'm afraid of those serious faces; I dislike them. I'm afraid of serious conversations. We'd be better off remaining silent.

LOPAKHIN: You know, I get up at five in the morning and work from dawn till night. I am always handling money, mine or someone else's, and I know what kind of people I deal with. It doesn't take much to see how few honest and decent people there are in the world. Sometimes, when I'm lying awake at night, I think: "O Lord, you have given us mighty forests, boundless fields, and immense horizons, and living here we should really be giants."

MADAME RANEVSKY: You actually want giants?! They're only good in fairy stories; but in real life they can be very frightening. *(Epihodov passes at the back of the scene, playing on his guitar)* There goes Epihodov.

ANYA: *(pensively)* There goes Epihodov.

GAYEV: The sun has set.

TROFIMOV: Yes.

GAYEV: *(as if declaiming, but not loud)* O Nature, divine Nature, you glow with eternal light; beautiful and indifferent. You whom we call our mother, combine in yourself both life and death, you give life and you destroy....

VARYA: *(entreatingly)* Uncle!

ANYA: You're at it again, uncle!

TROFIMOV: You'd be better off chipping the red into the center pocket.

GAYEV: I'll keep quiet! I'll keep quiet!

(They all sit pensively. Silence reigns, broken only by the mumbling of old Firs. Suddenly a distant sound is heard as if from the sky, the sound of a string breaking, dying away, melancholy.)

MADAME RANEVSKY: What was that?

LOPAKHIN: I don't know. Maybe a cable snapped in the mine and a bucket fell down a shaft. It must be very far away.

GAYEV: It might be a bird of some kind...a heron, or something.

TROFIMOV: Or an owl.

MADAME RANEVSKY: *(shuddering)* I don't know why, but it's awful!

FIRS: The same thing happened before the great catastrophe: the owl screeched and the samovar kept hissing.

GAYEV: What catastrophe?

FIRS: The emancipation. *(a pause)*

MADAME RANEVSKY: Come on, everybody, let's go in; it's getting late. *(to Anya)* You've got tears in your eyes. What is it, my little darling? *(embracing her)*

ANYA: Nothing, mamma. I'm all right.

TROFIMOV: Someone's coming.

(A Tramp appears in a torn white peaked cap and overcoat. He is slightly drunk.)

TRAMP: Excuse me, but can I come through here to the railroad station?

GAYEV: Of course. Just follow this path.

TRAMP: Deeply obliged to you, sir. *(coughing)* We're having wonderful weather. *(declaiming:)* "Brother, my suffering brother!... Come to the Volga. What is that groaning"... *(to Varya)* Mademoiselle, can you spare a few kopeks for a hungry Russian?

VARYA: *frightened, screams.*

LOPAKHIN: *(angrily)* There's a right way and a wrong way to do everything!

MADAME RANEVSKY: Here, take this. *(fumbling in her purse)* I don't have any silver.... Never mind, take this gold piece.

TRAMP: Deeply obliged to you, madam. *(exit Tramp; laughter)*

48

VARYA: *(frightened)* I'm going home! I'm going! Oh, mamma, the servants have nothing to eat, and you gave that man a gold piece.

MADAME RANEVSKY: What can be done with your silly mother? I'll give you everything I have when we get home. Yermolai Alekseyevich, lend me some more money.

LOPAKHIN: Of course.

MADAME RANEVSKY: Come on, everyone; it's time to go back. And Varya, the marriage is all settled. I wish you joy.

VARYA: *(through her tears)* It's not a thing to joke about, mamma.

LOPAKHIN: Get thee to a nunnery, Amelia, go!

GAYEV: My hands are shaking. It's been ages since I played a game of billiards.

LOPAKHIN: Amelia, you nymph, in thine orisons remember my sins.

MADAME RANEVSKY: Come on. It's almost time for supper.

VARYA: God, how he frightened me! My heart is simply pounding.

LOPAKHIN: Let me remind you, ladies and gentlemen: the cherry orchard will be sold on the twenty-second of August. Remember that, remember that! *(all exit except Trofimov and Anya)*

ANYA: *(laughing)* We should be thankful to the tramp for scaring Varya. At last we're alone.

TROFIMOV: Varya's afraid we'll fall in love with each other. She won't leave us alone. Her narrow mind can't grasp that we're above love. To eliminate everything petty and ephemeral, everything that stops us from being free and happy, that is the whole meaning and purpose of our life. Forward! We are moving irresistibly toward that bright star which burns in the distance! Forward! Don't hang back, my friends!

ANYA: *(clasping her hands)* What beautiful things you say! *(a pause)* Isn't it lovely here today!

TROFIMOV: Yes, the weather's wonderful.

ANYA: What have you done to me, Petya? Somehow I don't love the cherry orchard any more like I used to? I used to love it so much; I thought there was no better place on earth than our orchard.

TROFIMOV: All Russia is our orchard. The earth is large and beautiful; it is full of wonderful places. *(a pause)* Think, Anya, your grandfather, your great-grandfather, and all your ancestors were slave-owners, owners of living souls. Don't you see human spirits peering at you from every tree in the orchard, from every leaf, from every branch? Don't you hear their voices?...Oh, it's awful. Your orchard is a terrible thing. Possessing living souls has corrupted all of you, those who lived before and since. You, your mother, and your uncle don't know that you are living off other people, people who weren't even allowed in the house. When I walk through the orchard in the early evening or at night, the old bark on the trees glows dimly, and the old cherry trees seem to be dreaming of all the centuries gone. Well, well, we are at least two hundred years behind the times. We have achieved nothing at all yet; we haven't yet decided how to relate to the past. We only theorize, complain of boredom, or drink vodka. It's so obvious that, before we can live in the present, we must first redeem the past, and break with it. And we can only redeem it through suffering, only by relentless unceasing labor. Understand that, Anya.

ANYA: The house we live in has long since ceased to be our house; and I shall go away, I give you my word.

TROFIMOV: If you have the house keys, throw them into the well and leave. Be free, be free as the wind.

ANYA: *(enthusiastically)* How beautifully you say that!

TROFIMOV: Believe me, Anya, believe me. I'm not thirty yet; I'm still young, still a student, but I've gone through so much! I am hungry as the winter, sick, nervous, poor as a beggar. Fate has tossed me from one place to another. I have been everywhere, everywhere. But wherever I've gone, every minute of the day and night, my soul has been full of ominous foreboding. I sense the coming of happiness, Anya. I see glimpses of it already....

ANYA: *(pensively)* The moon is rising.

(Epihodov is heard still playing the same sad tune on his guitar. The moon rises. Somewhere beyond the poplar trees, Varya is heard calling for Anya: "Anya, where are you?")

TROFIMOV: Yes, the moon is rising. *(a pause)* Here it is, here comes happiness; it is moving toward us, closer and closer; I can hear its footsteps.... And if we do not see it, if we never get to know it, what does it matter? Others will see it after us.

51

VARYA: *(without)* Anya? Where are you?

TROFIMOV: Varya again! *(angrily)* It's so awful!

ANYA: Never mind. Let's go down to the river. It's lovely there.

TROFIMOV: Yes, let's go!

(exeunt Anya and Trofimov)

VARYA'S VOICE: Anya! Anya!

ACT 3

A sitting room separated by an arch from a large drawing room behind. Lighted chandelier. The Jewish orchestra mentioned in Act 2 is heard playing on the landing. Evening. In the drawing room they are dancing the grand rond. Pishchik is heard crying: "Promenade a une paire!" *The dancers come down into the sitting room. The first pair consists of Pishchik and Carlotta; the second of Trofimov and Madame Ranevsky; the third of Anya and the Post Office Clerk; the fourth of Varya and the Stationmaster, etc., etc. Varya is crying softly and wipes away the tears as she dances. In the last pair comes Dunyasha. They cross the sitting room.*

PISHCHIK: *Grand rond, balancez... Les cavaliers a genou et remerciez vos dames.*

(Firs in evening dress carries soda water across on a tray)

(Pishchik and Trofimov come down into the sitting room)

PISHCHIK: I'm a robust man, I've had two strokes already. Dancing is hard work, but, as the saying goes, "When you run with the pack, if you can't bark, at least wag your tail." I'm as strong as a horse. My old father, who loved to joke, God rest his soul, he used to say that the ancient line of Semyonov-Pishchiks was descended from Caligula's horse, the one he made a senator....

53

(sitting) But the trouble is, I have no money. A hungry dog thinks about nothing but meat. *(snoring and waking up again at once)* It's the same with me. I think about nothing but money.

TROFIMOV: You know, it's true, you do look like a horse.

PISHCHIK: Well, well...a horse is a fine animal... you can sell a horse.

(A sound of billiards being played in the next room. Varya apears in the drawing room beyond the arch.)

TROFIMOV: *(teasing her)* Madame Lopakhina. Madame Lopakhina.

VARYA: *(angrily)* Mangy gentleman!

TROFIMOV: Yes, I am a mangy gentleman, and I'm proud of it.

VARYA: *(bitterly)* We've hired the orchestra, but who has any money to pay for it? *(she exits)*

TROFIMOV: *(to Pishchik)* If you had saved just half the energy you spend looking to pay the interest on your loans and put it to some useful purpose, you'd have had enough money to turn the world upside down.

PISHCHIK: Nietzsche, the famous philosopher, a very remarkable thinker, a man of colossal intellect, says in his works that it's perfectly all right to forge banknotes.

TROFIMOV: Since when do you read Nietzsche?

PISHCHIK: Well...Dashenka told me....But I'm in such trouble now, I'd forge them in a minute. I have to pay three hundred ten rubles the day after tomorrow....I've only got one hundred thirty. *(feeling his pockets; alarmed)* Where's my money! I've lost my money! *(crying)* Where'd my money go? *(joyfully)* Here it is, inside the lining.... I'm sweating bullets.

(enter Madame Ranevsky and Carlotta)

MADAME RANEVSKY: *(humming a Lezginka)* Why is Leonid taking so long? What is he doing in town? *(to Dunyasha)* Dunyasha, ask the musicians if they'd like some tea.

TROFIMOV: It's probable the auction did not take place.

MADAME RANEVSKY: It was a stupid time to invite the musicians, it was a stupid time to have a dance.... Well, what does it matter.... *(she sits down and sings softly to herself)*

CARLOTTA: *(giving Pishchik a pack of cards)* This is a deck of cards. Think of any one you like.

PISHCHIK: I've got one.

CARLOTTA: Now shuffle. Very good. Now give them to me. Oh, most worthy Herr Pishchik. *Ein, zwei, drei!* Now look in your side pocket.

PISHCHIK: *(taking a card from his side pocket)* The eight of spades! That's it exactly. *(astonished)* Well, imagine that!

CARLOTTA: *(holding the pack on the palm of her hand, to Trofimov)* Tell me quickly, what card's on top?

TROFIMOV: The queen of spades?

CARLOTTA: Correct! *(to Pishchik)* Now you, what card's on top?

PISHCHIK: Ace of hearts?

CARLOTTA: Correct! *(she claps her hands; the pack of cards disappears)* What lovely weather we're having.

(A mysterious female voice answers her as if from under the door: "Oh yes, indeed, it's splendid weather, mademoiselle.")

CARLOTTA: You are my perfect ideal.

THE VOICE: I think you are also ferry peautiful, mademoiselle.

STATIONMASTER: *(applauding)* Bravo, Madame Ventriloquist!

PISHCHIK: *(astonished)* Well, imagine that! Bewitching Carlotta Ivanovna, I've fallen madly in love with you.

CARLOTTA: In love! *(shrugging her shoulders)* Are you capable of love? *Guter Mensch, aber schlechter Musikant!*

TROFIMOV: *(slapping Pishchik on the shoulder)* Good old horse!

CARLOTTA: Pay attention, please. One more trick. *(taking a shawl from a chair)* Now here's a very pretty shawl. I'm going to sell this very pretty shawl. *(shaking it)* Who wants to buy it?

PISHCHIK: *(astonished)* Well, that's something!

CARLOTTA: *Ein zwei, drei!* *(she lifts the shawl quickly, revealing Anya, who curtsies, runs to her mother, kisses her, then runs back into the drawing room amid general applause)*

MADAME RANEVSKY: *(applauding)* Bravo! bravo!

CARLOTTA: Once more. *Ein, zwei, drei!* *(she lifts up the shawl; behind it stands Varya, bowing)*

PISHCHIK: *(astonished)* Well, that is something!

56

CARLOTTA: The end. *(she throws the shawl over Pishchik, makes a curtsy, and runs up into the drawing room)*

PISHCHIK: *(hurrying after her)* You little minx . . . What a woman, what a woman. . . . *(he exits)*

MADAME RANEVSKY: And still no sign of Leonid. What he is doing in town all this time, I simply can't understand. It must be all over by now. Either the estate is sold or the auction never happened. Why does he keep me in such suspense?

VARYA: *(trying to soothe her)* Uncle has bought it, I'm sure of that.

TROFIMOV: *(mockingly)* Who could doubt it!

VARYA: Great-aunt sent him power of attorney to buy it in her name and transfer the mortgage. She's doing it for Anya's sake. I'm sure that God will help uncle to buy it.

MADAME RANEVSKY: Our great-aunt in Yaroslav sent fifteen thousand to buy the estate in her name— she doesn't trust us. But that's not enough to even pay the interest. *(covering her face with her hands)* Today my fate will be decided, my fate. . . .

TROFIMOV: *(teasing Varya)* Madame Lopakhina!

VARYA: *(angrily)* Perpetual student! Twice he's been kicked out of the university.

MADAME RANEVSKY: Why so angry, Varya? He's just teasing you about Lopakhin. So what? Go ahead and marry Lopakhin if you want to; he's a nice, interesting man. And if not, don't. Nobody's forcing you, darling.

VARYA: I'm very serious about this thing, mamma, if you want to know the truth. He's a good man and I like him.

MADAME RANEVSKY: Then marry him. Why put it off?

VARYA: Mamma, I can't do the proposing. It's two years now that people have been talking to me about him, everyone talks. But either he just keeps quiet or he cracks a joke. I can understand. He has to make money; he has to worry about business, he can't be bothered with me. If only I had some money, even a little, say a hundred rubles, I'd drop everything and leave. I'd enter a nunnery.

TROFIMOV: *(mocking)* Ecstasy!

VARYA: *(to Trofimov)* A student ought to have more intelligence. *(in a gentler voice, crying)* You've gotten so ugly, Petya; and so old! *(she stops crying; to Madame Ranevsky)* Mamma, I just can't live without work. I have to be working every minute of the day.

(enter Yasha)

YASHA: *(trying not to laugh)* Epihodov has broken a billiard cue. *(exit Yasha)*

VARYA: What's Epihodov doing here? Who gave him permission to play billiards? I don't understand these people. *(exit Varya)*

MADAME RANEVSKY: Don't tease her, Petya. Can't you see how unhappy she is already?

TROFIMOV: I wish she'd stop being such a pain in the neck, always meddling in other people's affairs. All summer she's been after Anya and me. She's afraid we'll fall in love. Is that any business of hers? You can be sure I never put that idea in her head. So banal. We're above love!

MADAME RANEVSKY: Then I must be beneath love. *(deeply agitated)* Where's Leonid? If only somebody would tell me whether the property's been sold or not! It all seems so impossible, I don't know what to think.... I'm all confused... I'm going to start screaming, I'll do something idiotic. Help me, Petya; say something to me, anything....

TROFIMOV: If the property is sold today or not, who cares? It was all over long ago; there's no turning back; the path is overgrown. Just stay calm, dear Lyubov Andreyevna. Don't lie to yourself any more. Once in your life look truth straight in the face.

MADAME RANEVSKY: What truth? You know what's true and what's not true, but I don't have that talent. I can see nothing. For you every question has an easy solution; but tell me, Petya, isn't that because you're young, because you've never suffered? You can look boldly ahead, but isn't that because you see nothing frightening in the future; because life is still hidden from your young eyes? You are more courageous, more honest, more profound than we are, but just for a minute be generous, show some pity for me. Don't you see? I was born here, my father and mother lived here, and my grandfather too. I love this house—without the cherry orchard my life would be nothing, and if it *must* be sold, then sell me with it, for God's sake! *(embracing Trofimov and kissing him on the forehead)* My little boy drowned here. *(crying)* Be gentle with me, dear, kind Petya.

TROFIMOV: You know my heart is full of sympathy for you.

MADAME RANEVSKY: Yes, I know, but you have a funny way of showing it. *(taking out her handkerchief and dropping a telegram)* I am so miserable today, you can't imagine! All this noise jars on my nerves, my heart jumps at every sound. I tremble all over, but I can't seclude myself; the silence terrifies me when I'm alone. Don't be hard on me, Petya; I love you like a son. I would gladly let Anya marry you, I swear it; but you must work, Petya. You must get your degree. You don't do anything; you're tossed around by fate from place to place; and that's not right. I'm telling the truth, no? And you must do something to make your beard grow. *(laughing)* You look so funny.

TROFIMOV: *(picking up the telegram)* I have no wish to look like an Adonis.

MADAME RANEVSKY: It's a telegram from Paris. I get them every day. One came yesterday, then today. That brute is sick again; he's in trouble again. . . . He begs me to forgive him, he begs me to come; and I really should go to Paris and be with him. You look at me so sternly; but what am I to do, Petya? What am I to do? He's sick, he's lonely, he's unhappy. Who will take care of him? Who will prevent him from doing stupid things? Who will give him his medicine on time? Look, why should I be ashamed to say it? I love him, there I've said it. I love him, I love him. . . . My love is like a stone tied round my neck; it's dragging me down to the bottom. But I love my stone. I can't live without it. *(squeezing Trofimov's hand)* Don't think badly of me, Petya. Just don't say anything! Don't say anything!

TROFIMOV: *(crying)* I'm sorry to be blunt, but, for God's sake, the man has robbed you.

60

MADAME RANEVSKY: No, no, no! *(stopping her ears)* Don't say that!

TROFIMOV: He's a scoundrel; everybody knows it but you. He's a petty scoundrel, a user....

MADAME RANEVSKY: *(angry but restrained)* You're twenty-six or twenty-seven, and you're still in the lower grades!

TROFIMOV: Who cares?

MADAME RANEVSKY: You ought to be grown up by now. At your age you ought to understand about love. You ought to love someone yourself, you ought to have an affair! *(angrily)* Yes, yes! You talk about purity, but you're just a prude, a crank, a freak....

TROFIMOV: *(horrified)* What is she saying?!!

MADAME RANEVSKY: "I'm above love!" You're not above love; you're simply what Firs calls a "good-for-nothing." It's a shame at your age you don't have a mistress!

TROFIMOV: *(aghast)* This is awful! What is she saying? *(going quickly up into the drawing room, clasping his head with his hands)* This is simply awful! Unbearable! I'm going.... *(exit, but returns at once)* It's all over between us!

MADAME RANEVSKY: *(exiting to landing and calling after him)* Stop, Pyotr! Don't be ridiculous; I was only joking! Pyotr!

(Trofimov is heard on the landing going quickly down the stairs, and suddenly falling down them with a crash. Anya and Varya scream. A moment later the sound of laughter.)

MADAME RANEVSKY: What happened? *(Anya runs in)*

ANYA: *(laughing)* Petya's fallen down the stairs. *(she runs out again)*

MADAME RANEVSKY: What a ridiculous person he is!

(The Stationmaster stands in the middle of the drawing room beyond the arch and recites Alexei Tolstoy's poem "The Sinner." Everyone stops to listen, but after a few lines the sound of a waltz is heard from the landing and he breaks off. All dance. Trofimov, Anya, Varya, and Madame Ranevsky enter from the landing.)

MADAME RANEVSKY: Come on, Petya, come on, you pure soul.... I apologize. Let's dance.

(She dances with Trofimov. Anya and Varya dance. Enter Firs, who puts his walking stick by the side door.)

YASHA: What's up, grandfather?

FIRS: I'm not feeling so good. In the old days it was generals and barons and admirals that danced at our balls. Now we send for the postmaster and the stationmaster, and even they're not eager to come. I'm feeling a little weak, somehow. The old master, their grandfather, used to give us all sealing wax when we felt sick. I've been taking sealing wax every day for twenty years. Even more. Maybe that's why I'm still alive.

YASHA: You're so boring, grandfather. *(yawning)* Why don't you drop dead and be done with it.

FIRS: Ech! you... good for nothing! *(he mumbles to himself)*
(Trofimov and Madame Ranevsky dance beyond the arch and down into the sitting room)

MADAME RANEVSKY: *Merci.* I'm going to sit down. *(sitting)* I'm tired.

(enter Anya)

62

ANYA: *(agitated)* Somebody was in the kitchen just now saying that the cherry orchard was sold today.

MADAME RANEVSKY: Sold? To whom?

ANYA: He didn't say who. He's gone. *(She dances with Trofimov. Both dance up into the drawing room.)*

YASHA: It was just some old fellow babbling; a stranger.

FIRS: And Leonid Andreyevich still isn't back. He's got on his light fall overcoat; he's sure to catch cold. Ah, these green kids!

MADAME RANEVSKY: This is killing me. Yasha, go and find out who bought it.

YASHA: But that old man's probably gone by now. *(laughs)*

MADAME RANEVSKY: *(vexed)* What are you laughing at? What makes you so happy?

YASHA: That Epihodov is so funny. A real idiot. Twenty-two misfortunes!

MADAME RANEVSKY: Where will you go if the estate is sold, Firs?

FIRS: Wherever you tell me, I'll go.

MADAME RANEVSKY: Why do you look like that? Are you sick? You should be in bed.

FIRS: *(ironically)* Oh yes, I'll go to bed, and who'll manage things, who'll give the orders? I have the whole house to take care of.

YASHA: Lyubov Andreyevna! Do me a favor please. If you go to Paris again, take me with you, won't you? It's completely impossible for me to stay here. *(looking about; sotto voce)* No need to say more. You can see for yourself. This country is uncivilized; the people have no morals; and the boredom! The food in the kitchen is inedible, and then old Firs creeps around mumbling all kinds of nonsense. Take me back with you, please!

(enter Pishchik)

PISHCHIK: Permit me the pleasure of a waltz, charming lady. *(Madame Ranevsky takes his arm)* And also, fair one, you must let me have one hundred eighty rubles. *(dancing)* Only one hundred eighty rubles.

(exeunt dancing through the arch)

YASHA: *(singing to himself)*
"Oh, canst thou understand
The unrest in my soul?"

(Beyond the arch appears a figure in grey top hat and checked trousers, jumping around and waving its arms. Cries of "Bravo, Carlotta Ivanovna.")

DUNYASHA: *(stopping to powder her face)* Miss Anya told me to dance—the gentlemen outnumber the ladies. But dancing makes me giddy and my heart goes pitter patter. Firs Nikolayevich, just now the post office clerk said something so nice to me it quite took my breath away. *(the music stops)*

FIRS: What did he say to you?

DUNYASHA: "You," he said, "are like a flower."

YASHA: *(yawning)* Idiot!

(exit Yasha)

DUNYASHA: Like a flower! I'm such a delicate creature, compliments make me tremble.

FIRS: Watch your step. You'll end up badly. *(enter Epihodov)*

EPIHODOV: You are not happy to see me, Avdotya Fyodorovna. I am no more to you than an insect. *(sighing)* Ah! Life! Life!

DUNYASHA: What do you want?

EPIHODOV: Unquestionably, perhaps, you are right. *(sighing)* But of course, if one sees it, so to speak, from a point of view, if you'll forgive the expression, and I apologize for my frankness, you have completely reduced me to a state of mind. I am aware of my destiny, every day some new misfortune, and I have long since become accustomed to it. Now I face my fate with a smile. But you did give me your word, and although I . . .

DUNYASHA: We can talk about this later, but now please leave me alone. I am busy thinking about other things. *(playing with her fan)*

EPIHODOV: Every day a new misfortune, and yet, if I may say so, I merely smile, and even laugh.

(enter Varya from the drawing room)

VARYA: *(to Epihodov)* You're not gone yet, Semyon? You never do what you're told. *(to Dunyasha)* You can go now, Dunyasha. *(to Epihodov)* First you play billiards and break a cue, then you tramp through the drawing room as if you were a guest!

EPIHODOV: Permit me to inform you that you have no right to tell me what to do.

VARYA: I'm not telling you what to do. I'm just talking to you about something. You do nothing but wander around from one place to another, and you never do a stroke of work. Why on earth we keep a clerk here no one knows.

EPIHODOV: *(offended)* Whether I work, or whether I wander around, or whether I eat or play billiards, these are questions to be decided only by my elders and people who understand things.

VARYA: *(furious)* How dare you talk to me like that! How dare you! You're saying I don't understand things? Get out of here this minute! Do you hear? This minute!

EPIHODOV: *(flinching)* I beg you to express your thoughts in more genteel language.

VARYA: *(beside herself)* You get out of here this instant! Get out! *(following him as he retreats toward the door)* Twenty-two misfortunes! Get out of my sight!

(exit Epihodov)

EPIHODOV: *(without)* I shall lodge a formal complaint against you.

VARYA: Oh, you're coming back, are you? *(seizing the walking stick left at the door by Firs)* Come on! Come on! Come on! I'll show you! Are you coming? Are you coming? Then take that. *(she brandishes the stick as Lopakhin enters)*

LOPAKHIN: Thank you very kindly.

VARYA: *(still angry, but ironical)* I beg your pardon.

LOPAKHIN: Not at all. I'm very grateful for your gracious welcome.

VARYA: No need to thank me. *(she walks away, then looks round and asks in a gentle voice)* Did I hurt you?

LOPAKHIN: Oh no, nothing worth mentioning. I'll have a big goose egg, that's all.

(Voices from the drawing room: "Lopakhin is here! Yermolai Alekseyevich!")

PISHCHIK: Let me take him in, as I live and breathe. *(he and Lopakhin kiss)* You smell of brandy, old man. We've been living it up here, too.

(enter Madame Ranevsky)

MADAME RANEVSKY: Is that you, Yermolai Alekseyevich? What took you so long? Where's Leonid?

LOPAKHIN: Leonid Andreyevich came back with me. He's on his way.

MADAME RANEVSKY: *(agitated)* Well, what happened? Did the sale take place? Tell me!

LOPAKHIN: *(embarrassed, afraid of revealing his joy)* The auction was over by four o'clock. We missed the train and had to wait till 9:30 *(sighing heavily)* Ouf! I'm a little dizzy....

(Enter Gayev. In one hand he carries parcels, with the other he wipes away his tears.)

MADAME RANEVSKY: What happened, Lyonya? Lyonya? *(impatiently, crying)* Quickly, quickly, for God's sake!

GAYEV: *(answering her only by waving his hand up and down; to Firs, crying)* Here, take these.... Here are some anchovies and Black Sea herrings. I haven't eaten all day. God, what I've been through! *(Through the open door of the billiard room comes the click of the billiard balls and Yasha's voice: "Seven, eighteen!" Gayev's expression changes; he stops crying.)* I'm awfully tired. Come and help me change, Firs. *(he goes up through the drawing room, Firs following)*

PISHCHIK: What about the auction? Come on, tell us.

MADAME RANEVSKY: Is the cherry orchard sold?

LOPAKHIN: Yes.

MADAME RANEVSKY: Who bought it?

LOPAKHIN: I did. *(A pause. Madame Ranevsky is overwhelmed by the news. She would fall to the ground but for the chair and table by her. Varya takes the keys from her belt, throws them on the floor in the middle of the sitting room, and exits.)* I bought it. Wait a minute; don't rush me. I'm all dizzy. I can't talk....*(laughing)* When we got to the auction, Deriganov was already there. Leonid Andreyevich had only fifteen thousand, and right away Deriganov bid thirty thousand more than the mortgage. After I checked things out, I bumped him up to forty. He came back with forty-five. I bid fifty-five. He kept raising five thousand, you see, while I went up ten.... Well, it didn't last much longer. I bid ninety thousand more than the mortgage, and the gavel sounded, and now the cherry orchard is mine! Mine! *(laughing)* God! God in heaven. The cherry orchard's mine! Tell me I'm drunk. Tell me I'm out of mind. Tell me I'm dreaming!...*(stamping his feet)* Don't laugh at me! If only my father and grandfather could rise from their graves and see what's happened, how their Yermolai, their half-literate, beaten Yermolai, who used to run around barefoot in winter, how that same Yermolai has bought a beautiful estate that has no equal in the whole entire world! I have bought the place where my father and grandfather were slaves, where they weren't even allowed in the kitchen. I'm fast asleep, it's only a dream, it can't be real... "'Tis the fruit of imagination wrapped in the mists of uncertainty." *(picking up the keys and smiling affectionately)* She threw away her keys, she wants to show she's not the mistress here any more.... *(jingling them together)* Well, well, it doesn't matter. *(the musicians are heard tuning up)* Hey, musicians, play! I want to hear some music. Come on everybody and see how Yermolai Lopakhin will lay his axe to the cherry orchard. Come and see the trees fall down! We'll fill the place with summer cottages, and our grandsons and great-grandsons will see a new life here....Strike up the music! *(The band plays. Madame Ranevsky sinks into a chair and weeps bitterly.)* *(reproachfully)* Oh why didn't you listen to me, why? You can't turn back the clock now, poor dear. *(crying)* Oh, if only all this were over! If only our confused unhappy life could change!

PISHCHIK: *(taking him by the arm, sotto voce)* She's crying. Let's go into the drawing room and leave her alone....Come on. *(taking him by the arm and going up toward the drawing room)*

LOPAKHIN: What's happening? Musicians, play so I can hear you! Everything has to suit me now. *(ironically)* Here comes the new master, the new owner of the cherry orchard! *(knocking by accident against a table and nearly tipping over the candelabra)* Never mind, I can pay for everything!

(Exit with Pishchik. Nobody remains in the drawing room or sitting room except Madame Ranevsky, who sits huddled up, weeping bitterly. The band plays softly. Enter Anya and Trofimov quickly. Anya goes to her

mother and kneels before her. Trofimov stands in the entry to the drawing room.)

ANYA: Mamma! You're crying, mamma. My dear, kind, sweet mamma! My darling, I love you! I bless you! The cherry orchard is sold, it's gone, that's true, quite true. But don't cry, mamma, you've still got your life before you, you've still got your pure and lovely soul. Come with me, my darling; come away from here. We'll plant a new orchard, even lovelier than this one. You will see it and understand, and joy, deep, tranquil joy will sink down upon your soul like a sunset, and you will smile, mamma. Come, darling, come, come!

ACT 4

Same scene as Act 1. There are no curtains, no pictures. The little furniture left is stacked in a corner, as if for sale. A feeling of emptiness. By the door to the hall and at the back of the scene are piled suitcases, bundles, etc. The door is open and the voices of Varya and Anya are audible. Lopakhin stands waiting. Yasha holds a tray with small tumblers of champagne. Epihodov is tying up a box in the hall. A distant murmur of voices behind the scene; the peasants have come to say goodbye.

GAYEV: *(without)* Thank you, my friends, thank you.

YASHA: The peasants have come to say goodbye. They're good fellows, Yermolai Alekseyevich, but in my opinion a little stupid.

(The murmur of voices dies away. Enter Madame Ranevsky and Gayev from the hall. She is not crying, but she is pale, her face twitches, and she cannot speak.)

GAYEV: You gave them everything in your purse, Lyuba. That was wrong, quite wrong!

MADAME RANEVSKY: I couldn't help it, I couldn't help it!

(exeunt both)

LOPAKHIN: *(calling after them through the doorway)* Won't you please come here and drink a glass as a goodbye?—I didn't bring any champagne from

71

town, and I only found one bottle at the station. Please, come back. *(a pause)* Won't you join me, my friends? *(returning from the door)* I wouldn't have bought it if I'd known. Well, then, I won't drink either. *(Yasha sets the tray down carefully on a chair)* Have a glass yourself, Yasha.

YASHA: Here's to our departure! Good luck! *(drinking)* This isn't the good champagne, you can be sure of that.

LOPAKHIN: Eight rubles a bottle. *(a pause)* God, it's cold in here.

YASHA: They didn't light the stoves today since we're all going away. *(he laughs)*

LOPAKHIN: Why are you laughing?

YASHA: I'm just amused.

LOPAKHIN: It's already October, but outside it's as calm and sunny as summer. Good weather for building. *(looking at his watch and speaking off)* Don't forget, ladies and gentlemen, that the train leaves in exactly forty-seven minutes. That means you have twenty minutes before you start for the station. Not much time!

(enter Trofimov in an overcoat, from outside)

TROFIMOV: Seems like time we were leaving. The carriages are here. Where the devil are my galoshes? They're lost. *(calling off)* Anya, my galoshes are missing. I can't find them anywhere!

LOPAKHIN: I have to go to Kharkov. I'll be taking the same train. I'm going to spend the winter in Kharkov. I've been hanging around with you people all this time, and I'm sick and tired of loafing. I can't live without work, I don't know what to do with my hands; they dangle about as if they don't belong to me.

TROFIMOV: Well, we'll be gone soon, and you can go back to your blessed labors.

LOPAKHIN: Have a glass.

TROFIMOV: Not me.

LOPAKHIN: So you're off to Moscow?

TROFIMOV: Yes, I'll see them into town, then go on to Moscow tomorrow.

LOPAKHIN: Well, well...I guess the professors haven't started their lectures yet. They've been waiting for you to arrive.

TROFIMOV: That's none of your business!

LOPAKHIN: How many years have you been going to the university?

TROFIMOV: Try and think of a new joke. That one's getting stale. *(looking for his galoshes)* Look, we'll probably never meet again, so let me give you a bit of free advice: Don't flap your hands around! Get out of the habit of waving your arms. Building cottages and announcing that the summer residents will turn into permanent owners, all that is flapping too. In spite of everything, I like you. You have fine, delicate fingers, like an artist. You have the delicate soul of an artist.

LOPAKHIN: *(embracing him)* Goodbye, dear fellow. Thank you for everything. Let me give you some money for the journey.

TROFIMOV: What for? I don't need it.

LOPAKHIN: But you don't have any.

TROFIMOV: Yes, I do. Thanks. I got some for a translation. Here it is, in my pocket. *(anxiously)* But I can't find my galoshes anywhere!

VARYA: *(from the next room)* Take the nasty things! *(she throws a pair of galoshes on the stage)*

TROFIMOV: Why are you so cranky, Varya? Hm... But those are not my galoshes!

LOPAKHIN: In the spring I harvested three thousand acres of poppies and now I've netted forty thousand rubles. When my poppies were in bloom, what a picture they made! So you see, I cleared forty thousand rubles; which means I can afford to lend you a bit. Don't be snobbish? I'm a peasant.... I don't hide my feelings.

TROFIMOV: Your father was a peasant, mine was a pharmacist. What does that prove? *(Lopakhin takes out his wallet)* Stop, stop, don't.... If you offered me two hundred thousand I wouldn't take it. I'm a free man. All the things you value so highly, both rich and poor, don't hold the slightest power over me. They're like feathers floating on the wind. I can live without you; I can go past you; I'm strong and proud. Mankind marches forward to the highest truth, to the greatest happiness possible on earth, and I am in the foremost ranks.

LOPAKHIN: Will you get there?

TROFIMOV: Yes. *(a pause)* I'll get there or I'll show others the way.

(the sound of axes chopping trees is heard in the distance)

LOPAKHIN: Well, goodbye, dear fellow, it's time to go. Here we are getting touchy with each other,

74

while life goes on without paying any attention to us. When I work for a long time without stopping, my mind relaxes and I think I know why I exist. But God alone knows why most of the Russian people exist.... Well, who cares? That doesn't keep the wheels turning. They say Leonid Andreyevich has got a job in a bank for six thousand a year.... He won't stay at it, he's too lazy.

ANYA: *(in the doorway)* Mamma asks that you not start chopping down the orchard until she's gone.

TROFIMOV: Really, don't you have any tact? *(exit Trofimov by the hall)*

LOPAKHIN: Of course, I'll stop them right away. What a bunch of idiots! *(exit after Trofimov)*

ANYA: Has Firs been taken to the hospital?

YASHA: I told them this morning. They must have sent him.

ANYA: *(to Epihodov, who crosses)* Simyon Panteleyevich, please find out if Firs has been taken to the hospital.

YASHA: *(offended)* I told Yegor this morning. Why ask a dozen times?

EPIHODOV: It is my considered opinion that our antiquarian friend is beyond repair. It's time he joined the ranks of his forefathers. I can only say I envy him. *(putting down a suitcase on a bandbox and crushing it flat)* There you are! You see? I knew it!

YASHA: *(jeering)* Twenty-two misfortunes! *(he exits)*

VARYA: *(without)* Has Firs been taken to the hospital?

ANYA: Yes.

VARYA: Then why did they leave the letter to the doctor?

ANYA: We must send it after them. *(she exits)*

VARYA: *(from the next room)* Where's Yasha? Tell him his mother's here to say goodbye.

YASHA: *(with a gesture of impatience)* They can really get on your nerves!

(Dunyasha has been busying herself with the luggage. Seeing Yasha alone, she approaches him.)

DUNYASHA: You could really look at me once, Yasha. You're going away, leaving me behind. *(crying and throwing her arms round his neck)*

YASHA: What's the use of crying? *(drinks champagne)* In six days I'll be back in Paris. Tomorrow we're off on the express, and goodbye to us! I can hardly believe it. *Vive la France!* This is no place for me. I can't stand it. . . . It can't be helped. I've had enough vulgarity, I'm fed up with it. *(drinking champagne)* What's the use of crying? Watch your morals, and you won't have to cry.

DUNYASHA: *(powdering her face and looking into a glass)* Write me a letter from Paris. I loved you, Yasha, I loved you a lot! I'm such a delicate creature, Yasha.

YASHA: There's somebody coming. *(he busies himself with the luggage, singing under his breath)*

(enter Madame Ranevsky, Gayev, Anya, and Carlotta)

GAYEV: We'll have to go; it's almost time. *(looking at Yasha)* Who smells of herring?

MADAME RANEVSKY: We have ten minutes to take our seats. *(looking round the room)* Goodbye, dear old house, dear old family home! Winter will pass and spring will come again, and you won't be here any more; they will tear you down. Just think of what these walls have seen! *(kissing Anya passionately)* My treasure, you look radiant, your eyes flash like diamonds. Are you happy? Very happy?

ANYA: Very, very happy. A new life is beginning, mamma.

GAYEV: *(gaily)* You know, she's right, everything is fine now. Until the cherry orchard was sold we were all anxious and miserable; but when the thing was finally settled once and for all, everybody calmed down and got more cheerful. I'm a bank clerk now; I'm a financier...red in the center pocket! And you, Lyuba, whatever you say, you're looking much much better, not a doubt about it.

MADAME RANEVSKY: Yes, my nerves are calmer; that's quite true. *(she is helped on with her hat and coat)* I'm sleeping well now. Take my things, Yasha. It's time to be off. *(to Anya)* We'll see each other soon, darling.... I'll go to Paris and live on the money your great-aunt sent from Yaroslav for the estate. God bless Great-aunt! But the money won't last long.

ANYA: You'll be back very very soon, won't you, mamma? I'll study hard and pass my high school exams, find a job and help you. We'll read all sorts of books together, won't we, mamma? *(kissing her mother's hands)* We'll read in the long autumn evenings, we'll read lots of books, and a whole new, wonderful world will open up before us. *(meditating)*...Come back, mamma!

MADAME RANEVSKY: I'll be back, my angel. *(embracing her)*

(enter Lopakhin; Carlotta sings softly)

GAYEV: Happy Carlotta, she's singing.

CARLOTTA: *(petting a bundle of rugs, like a swaddled baby)* Rock-a-bye, baby, on the tree top... *(the baby answers, "Wah, wah.")* Hush, my little one, hush, my pretty one! *("Wah, wah")* Don't break your mother's heart. *(she throws the bundle down on the floor again)* You simply must find me a new position. Please. I can't go on like this.

LOPAKHIN: We'll find you a place, Carlotta Ivanovna, don't you worry.

GAYEV: Everyone's deserting us. Varya's going away. Nobody seems to need us.

CARLOTTA: I have nowhere to live in town. I have to go. *(hums a tune)* It's all the same. It's all the same.

(enter Pishchik)

LOPAKHIN: Nature's masterpiece!

PISHCHIK: *(panting)* Oh my, let me catch my breath! ...I'm all in!...Noble friends!...Give me some water.

GAYEV: Wants some money, I'll bet. Excuse me, I'm getting out of here. *(he exits)*

PISHCHIK: I haven't seen you in ages, fairest lady. *(to Lopakhin)* You here? Glad to see you, you giant of intellect. Take this; it's for you. *(giving Lopakhin money)* Four hundred rubles! I still owe eight hundred forty.

LOPAKHIN: *(amazed, shrugging his shoulders)* I must be dreaming! Where did you get this?

PISHCHIK: Wait a minute.... I'm hot.... A most extraordinary thing! Some Englishmen came and found some kind of white clay on my land. *(to Madame Ranevsky)* And here's four hundred for you, lovely, marvelous lady. *(giving her money)* The rest another time. *(drinking water)* A minute ago a young man in the train was saying that some... some great philosopher recommends we jump off roofs.... Jump, he says, and solve the problem of life. *(with an astonished air)* Think of that! More water!

LOPAKHIN: Who were those Englishmen?

PISHCHIK: I leased them the plot with the clay on it for twenty-four years. But I've run out of time.... I must be running along. I'm going to Znoikov's, to Kardamonov's.... I owe everybody money. *(drinking)* Goodbye to you all; I'll drop by on Thursday.

MADAME RANEVSKY: We're just moving into town, and tomorrow I go abroad.

PISHCHIK: What! *(alarmed)* Why are you going to town? What's happened to all the furniture?... Suitcases?... Forget about it. *(crying)* It's all right. People of great intellect, those Englishmen. Never mind. Be happy... God will help you... it's all right. Everything in this world has to come to an end. *(kissing Madame Ranevsky's hand)* If word ever reaches you that my end has come, remember the old... horse, and say, "Once there lived a certain Semyonov Pishchik, God rest his soul." ... Remarkable weather we're having.... Yes.... *(goes out deeply moved; returns at once and says from the doorway)* Dashenka sends her regards. *(he exits)*

MADAME RANEVSKY: Now we can go. Only two things remain on my mind. One is poor old

FIRS. *(looking at her watch)* We still have five minutes.

ANYA: Firs has already gone to the hospital, mamma. Yasha sent him there this morning.

MADAME RANEVSKY: My second worry is Varya. She always gets up early to work, and now there's nothing to do. She's like a fish out of water. She's grown thin and pale and cries all the time, poor dear....*(a pause)* Yermolai Alekseyevich, you know I always hoped...to see her marry you, and I imagine you're looking for a wife. *(she whispers to Anya, who nods to Carlotta, and both exeunt)* She loves you, you seem fond of her, and I can't understand why you always avoid each other. I can't understand it.

LOPAKHIN: To tell you the truth, I don't understand it myself. It's all so strange. If there's still time I'll do it right now. Let's get it over with—and soon. Without you here, I'll never be able to propose to her.

MADAME RANEVSKY: A wonderful idea! It really doesn't take more than a minute. I'll call her in right now.

LOPAKHIN: And we even have the champagne ready. *(looking at the glasses)* Empty. Somebody's finished it. *(Yasha coughs)* That's what I call greedy!

MADAME RANEVSKY: *(animated)* Wonderful! We'll all leave you alone....*Allez*, Yasha. I'll call her. *(at the door)* Varya, leave all that alone and come here. Come quickly! *(exeunt Madame Ranevsky and Yasha)*

LOPAKHIN: *(looking at his watch)* Yes.

(A pause. A stifled laugh behind the door; whispering; at last Varya enters.)

80

VARYA: *(looking over the luggage)* That's strange; I can't seem to find it anywhere.

LOPAKHIN: What are you looking for?

VARYA: I packed it myself, and I can't remember. *(a pause)*

LOPAKHIN: Where are you going now, Varvara Mikhailovna?

VARYA: Me? To the Ragulins. I'm supposed to go and keep house for them, to be a housekeeper or something.

LOPAKHIN: Oh, at Yashnevo? That's about fifty miles from here. *(a pause)* Well, life in this house is over now.

VARYA: *(looking at the luggage)* Where can it be? Maybe I put it in the trunk.... Yes, life here is over now. There won't be any more...

LOPAKHIN: And I'm off to Kharkov... on the same train. I have a lot of business to do. I'm leaving Epihodov to look after this place. I've taken him on.

VARYA: Have you?

LOPAKHIN: Last year at this time snow was falling already, if you remember; but now it's fine and sunny. But it's still pretty cold anyway. Three degrees of frost.

VARYA: I didn't look. *(a pause)* Besides, our thermometer's broken. *(a pause)*

A VOICE: *(at the outer door)* Yermolai Alekseyevich!

LOPAKHIN: *(as if he had only been waiting to be called)* I'm coming! *(exit Lopakhin quickly)*

81

(Varya sits on the floor, puts her head on a bundle, and sobs softly. The door opens and Madame Ranevsky comes in cautiously.)

MADAME RANEVSKY: Well? *(a pause)* We have to go.

VARYA: *(no longer crying, wiping her eyes)* Yes, it's time, mamma. I'll be able to reach the Ragulins today, as long as I don't miss the train.

MADAME RANEVSKY: *(calling off)* Put on your things, Anya.

(Enter Anya, then Gayev and Carlotta. Gayev wears a warm overcoat with a hood. The servants and drivers come in. Epihodov busies himself with the luggage.)

MADAME RANEVSKY: Now we can start our journey.

ANYA: *(delighted)* We can start our journey!

GAYEV: My friends, my dear, beloved friends! Now that I'm leaving this house forever, can I keep silent? Must I refrain from expressing those emotions which at such a moment fill my whole being?

ANYA: *(pleadingly)* Uncle!

VARYA: Uncle, darling, what's the use?

GAYEV: *(sadly)* Double the red off the white in the center pocket. I'll keep quiet.

(enter Trofimov, then Lopakhin)

TROFIMOV: Come on everybody, it's time to go.

LOPAKHIN: Epihodov, my coat.

MADAME RANEVSKY: I'll just sit here one minute more. It's like I'd never noticed before what the walls of this house were like, or the ceilings. I look at them now with such hunger, with such tender love. . . .

GAYEV: I remember when I was six years old, how I sat on this window sill and watched my father starting out for church on Trinity Sunday.

MADAME RANEVSKY: Have they taken everything?

LOPAKHIN: Apparently everything. *(to Epihodov, putting on his overcoat)* Make sure everything's in order, Epihodov.

EPIHODOV: *(in a hoarse voice)* You can trust me, Yermolai Alekseyevich.

LOPAKHIN: What's wrong with your voice?

EPIHODOV: Just had a glass of water. Must've swallowed something.

YASHA: *(contemptuously)* Idiot!

MADAME RANEVSKY: We're going, and not a soul will be here after we're gone.

LOPAKHIN: Until spring.

(Varya pulls an umbrella out of a bundle of rugs, as if she were brandishing it to hit someone. Lopakhin pretends to be frightened.)

VARYA: Don't be silly! I had no intention...

TROFIMOV: Ladies and gentlemen, into the carriages. It's time to go. The train is coming this minute.

VARYA: There are your galoshes, Petya, by that suitcase. *(crying)* And what grubby old things they are!

TROFIMOV: *(putting on his galoshes)* Let's go.

GAYEV: *(much moved, afraid of crying)* The train... the station... double the red in the center; pot the white in the corner....

MADAME RANEVSKY: Let's go!

GAYEV: Are we all here? No one in there? *(locking the door)* There are some things stacked in there; I have to lock them up. Let's go!

ANYA: Goodbye, home! Goodbye to the old life!

TROFIMOV: Hello to the new life!

(Exit with Anya. Varya looks round the room, and exits slowly. Exeunt Yasha and Carlotta with her dog.)

LOPAKHIN: Until the spring, then. Goodbye my friends, until we meet again!

(Exit. Madame Ranevsky and Gayev are left alone. They seem to have been waiting for this, and throw their arms round each other's necks, sobbing restrainedly and gently, afraid of being overheard.)

GAYEV: *(in despair)* My sister! my sister!

MADAME RANEVSKY: Oh, my dear, sweet, lovely orchard! My life, my youth, my happiness, farewell! Farewell!

ANYA: *(calling gaily, without)* Mamma!

TROFIMOV: *(gay and excited)* Aa-oo!

MADAME RANEVSKY: One last look at these walls, these windows.... Dear mother used to love to walk about in this room.

GAYEV: My sister! my sister!

ANYA: *(without)* Mamma!

TROFIMOV: *(without)* Aa-oo!

MADAME RANEVSKY: We're coming.

(Exeunt. The stage is empty. Sound of all the doors being locked and the carriages driving away. All is quiet. Amid the silence the thud of an axe on a tree

echoes sad and lonely. The sound of footsteps. Firs appears in the doorway, from the right. He is dressed, as always, in his long coat and white waistcoat; he wears slippers. He is ill.)

FIRS: *(going to the door left and trying the handle)* Locked. They've gone. *(sitting on the sofa)* They've forgotten me. Never mind! I'll just sit here for a minute. I don't doubt Leonid Andreyevich put on his cloth coat instead of the fur. *(he sighs anxiously)* And I wasn't around to watch. Young wood, green wood! *(he mumbles something incomprehensible)* Life has passed me by as if I'd never lived. *(lying down)* I'll lie down for a minute. There's no strength left in you; nothing, nothing. Ech, you . . . good-for-nothing!

(He lies motionless. A distant sound is heard, as if from the sky, the sound of a string breaking, dying away, melancholy. Then silence, broken only by the thud of an axe on the trees far away in the cherry orchard.)

ELEPHANT PAPERBACKS

Theatre and Drama

Robert Brustein, *Dumbocracy in America*, EL421
Robert Brustein, *Reimagining American Theatre*, EL410
Robert Brustein, *The Theatre of Revolt*, EL407
Irina and Igor Levin, *Working on the Play and the Role*, EL411
Plays for Performance:
  Aristophanes, *Lysistrata*, EL405
  Pierre Augustin de Beaumarchais, *The Marriage of Figaro*,
    EL418
  Anton Chekhov, *The Cherry Orchard*, EL420
  Anton Chekhov, *The Seagull*, EL407
  Fyodor Dostoevsky, *Crime and Punishment*, EL416
  Euripides, *The Bacchae*, EL419
  Georges Feydeau, *Paradise Hotel*, EL403
  Henrik Ibsen, *Ghosts*, EL401
  Henrik Ibsen, *Hedda Gabler*, EL413
  Henrik Ibsen, *The Master Builder*, EL417
  Henrik Ibsen, *When We Dead Awaken*, EL408
  Heinrich von Kleist, *The Prince of Homburg*, EL402
  Christopher Marlowe, *Doctor Faustus*, EL404
  The Mysteries: Creation, EL412
  The Mysteries: The Passion, EL414
  Sophocles, *Electra*, EL415
  August Strindberg, *The Father*, EL406

ELEPHANT PAPERBACKS

Literature and Letters
Stephen Vincent Benét, *John Brown's Body*, EL10
Isaiah Berlin, *The Hedgehog and the Fox*, EL21
Robert Brustein, *Dumbocracy in America*, EL421
Anthony Burgess, *Shakespeare*, EL27
Philip Callow, *Son and Lover: The Young D. H. Lawrence*, EL14
James Gould Cozzens, *Castaway*, EL6
James Gould Cozzens, *Men and Brethren*, EL3
Clarence Darrow, *Verdicts Out of Court*, EL2
Floyd Dell, *Intellectual Vagabondage*, EL13
Theodore Dreiser, *Best Short Stories*, EL1
Joseph Epstein, *Ambition*, EL7
André Gide, *Madeleine*, EL8
Gerald Graff, *Literature Against Itself*, EL35
John Gross, *The Rise and Fall of the Man of Letters*, EL18
Irving Howe, *William Faulkner*, EL15
Aldous Huxley, *After Many a Summer Dies the Swan*, EL20
Aldous Huxley, *Ape and Essence*, EL19
Aldous Huxley, *Collected Short Stories*, EL17
Sinclair Lewis, *Selected Short Stories*, EL9
William L. O'Neill, ed., *Echoes of Revolt: The Masses,
     1911–1917*, EL5
Ramón J. Sender, *Seven Red Sundays*, EL11
Peter Shaw, *Recovering American Literature*, EL34
Wilfrid Sheed, *Office Politics*, EL4
Tess Slesinger, *On Being Told That Her Second Husband Has
     Taken His First Lover, and Other Stories*, EL12
B. Traven, *The Bridge in the Jungle*, EL28
B. Traven, *The Carreta*, EL25
B. Traven, *The Cotton-Pickers*, EL32
B. Traven, *General from the Jungle*, EL33
B. Traven, *Government*, EL23
B. Traven, *March to the Montería*, EL26
B. Traven, *The Night Visitor and Other Stories*, EL24
B. Traven, *The Rebellion of the Hanged*, EL29
Anthony Trollope, *Trollope the Traveller*, EL31
Rex Warner, *The Aerodrome*, EL22
Thomas Wolfe, *The Hills Beyond*, EL16

NEW HANOVER COUNTY PUBLIC LIBRARY
201 Chestnut Street
Wilmington, N.C. 28401

GAYLORD S